The Wisdom of Epinoia

A spiritual journey to find forgiveness

A book of modern-day parables

by Mark K. Laux

The Wisdom of Epinoia:
A spiritual journey to find forgiveness
Copyright © 2022 by Mark K. Laux

The story, all names, characters, and incidents
portrayed in this production are fictitious.

No identification with actual persons (living or deceased),
places, buildings, and products are intended or should
be inferred.

Book Cover by Sadie Butterworth-Jones

Like Helen, I know this is all true,
but I don't believe a word of it.

Contents

Chapter 1.

Magic Mirrors

While I was living, I never thought my life was very interesting. Most of my time was spent asking my wife to repeat herself, and my kids to shut the hell up. The entire experience blended together like a poorly written soap opera — just a bunch of days stuck together like a pile of cold, wet spaghetti in a colander. My wife would tell you different. She would say I kept her laughing. She would say I was an established artist, and that I helped her grow spiritually. That I was a good father, and a businessman who provided pretty well for his family. She would say I was intelligent and well-read. At least, that's what she said in my obituary; what she actually thinks may be altogether different. Just because I'm dead doesn't mean I'm able to read minds — and if you're wondering, no, I can't watch you do embarrassing stuff, either. But for a moment, after my death, I was able to bounce around the world of the living, which is how I came to read my own obituary.

Honestly, if I were still alive, I wouldn't have disagreed with her opinion of me anyway. To do so would only have led to an argument, with her telling me if I didn't think my life was interesting, to change it. She'd said that many times, even knowing full well that our lives were pasted together like two popsicle sticks with Elmer's glue. Besides, I couldn't disagree with her now anyway since I'm dead. Well, not dead, actually — just no longer holding my previous form, or in a body, or, I don't know, a sack of water walking around on a little blue marble in space. I guess now I'm formless content? Dead to anyone still in a body, though, that's for sure. Except I'm still aware. Maybe I'm awareness without form? I can still pull form together, but it doesn't feel right, and when I do that, I just look like a ghost, all shimmery and transparent — which is ironic, given I used to tell people that I was so white, I was nearly transparent. But that was back when I had a body, and only at the beach or a pool, to get out of taking off my shirt and exposing my "dad body." Pride — that's one thing about having a body I do not miss.

Another reason I don't see my previous life as very interesting is because I spent so much time meditating, which is just sitting on a mat for long periods, trying to think of nothing while breathing deeply. On the plus side, those meditations led to some seeming out-of-body experiences that I could barely describe or even understand. But every time that happened, my ego would rush in like a small dog chasing a mail truck, and the moment would be over, and I'd be left wondering what had just happened. I remember thinking, *What the hell was that?*, without getting an answer.

Then, when I got hit by the bus (I know, right? Didn't see that coming — literally — and the irony of that event isn't lost on me, either, because I would often tell people that when the cosmic bus comes by, get on, or it will run you down), I found myself in this room full of magic mirrors. At first, I thought I was in a hospital room, with all the shiny stuff they have. But no, it was a room of crazy mirrors — bright rectangles with people standing in front of them, looking into the mirrors and watching themselves do stuff. To get a better idea, imagine a huge sports bar, but the TVs are all turned on their sides and standing on the floor, about the height of a person, each playing a unique movie while someone in a bathrobe-like gown stands before it, mesmerized, completely lost in their own little world. They're all perfectly still, just standing there. It's like they're in a trance, dreaming with their eyes open.

The space — something like being in a house of mirrors in a carnival sideshow — was infinite. When I looked in any direction, the mirrors just went on and on. At first, I tried to see myself in the mirrors, thinking everything was a reflection, but I couldn't — or at least, not what I expected to see (not to mention that I didn't have a body anymore). What I expected was a middle-aged bald man with a paunch. Instead, I saw a bunch of little movies reflecting all the different people standing in front of their magic mirrors. It was as if their thoughts were being projected as a video, and they were the star by their own casting.

I wandered around the mirrors, (TVs?) for some time, which is a little misleading, since I couldn't walk, not having a body with legs. But I was able to move about easily. At first, it was like what people who have said near death experiences are like. I saw my closest friends and family members that had died before me and felt the kind of love you can only experience from those nearest to you.

This went on for some time until I started to have questions. Why was I here, in a space of magic mirrors? My dead friends and family didn't seem that real to me, and I couldn't figure out why. Plus, I had this gnawing feeling like I was missing something. Where was God in all of this? Was there a God? If yes, why didn't He, or She, or It show Itself? A flood of questions and odd feelings came over me. Imagine having sadness, guilt, shame, worry, fear, and nostalgia all blended in a food processor and drinking it like a smoothie, only not a sweet smoothie, but something sour. That, and I kept getting this thought about seeing things differently, but I couldn't get a clear idea of what I should be looking at, or what it meant. The words *sight and seeing* kept popping up, but seeing what?

Sightseeing? Was I headed somewhere? A museum of some kind? An art gallery? I always liked going to museums in my so-called life, but this felt different than the excitement of going to a museum or gallery. I felt anticipation, but not in a good way. This didn't seem like a vacation adventure at all. Instead, it felt more like a classroom the moment before taking a test I hadn't studied well for and was late for class. What I had thought might be a trip to heaven started to turn into confusion.

That is, until a woman named Epinoia stepped out from behind one of the mirrors. She apologized for being late and giggled. I know her name because she told me. My formless mind looked at her blankly for some time — which is a little misleading, because in the room of magic mirrors, time isn't linear, but sort of happens all at once. Anyway, it seemed like a moment passed, and then I asked her what her name is, and she told me. When I was a person in a body, bouncing around in the lost dream we think of as life, time seemed to start at one point and lead to another. Like when you put a pizza in the oven, you set the timer for fifteen to twenty minutes (oven temperatures vary; your times may be different), and over that time, the pizza cooks. Damn, I miss pizza! Epinoia tells me I can go back into a body and have pizza again if I'd like, but to keep in mind it's all imagined and can only lead to fear, sadness, and loss. Back to the pizza example: time starts with a frozen pizza and ends with a cooked pizza. But here, in the magic house of mirrors, time doesn't move from one point to another.

The pizza is frozen, cooked, eaten, not eaten, is a pizza, and isn't a pizza, all at once.

You may be wondering what Epinoia looks like. I'm not going to describe her to you, because if you ever get to the house of magic mirrors, she may look different for you. She may not even *be* a she. So, just think of an angel, be it male or female, and that will work. We're all just making this stuff up anyway, so looks are only important in keeping us in our imagined world. You see, the thing is, I could tell you that Epinoia is pretty, a certain height and shape with a specific skin color, and you may get an image of a pretty person in your mind, but you would be mistaken; she looks nothing like what you're thinking. Instead, she is an experience. She is a wave of love so deep that it cannot be defined. And with her love came great knowledge, that promised the answer to every remaining question I had about my former life in a body.

The first question I had was, why does she giggle so much? Every few seconds, she lets out a half-suppressed laugh. She smiled and replied, "It's Joy bubbling up. Joy, Love, Happiness, and Jubilation come in waves when we are co-creating with what you call God. The creation process is a giggle at this moment because you're just remembering what that's like." Noting my blank stare, she added, "You know — to create Love, to expand God's Gift." Then she giggled again. "Oh, my lovely brother, you'll understand quickly enough."

In my previous life I was a bit of a foul mouth. My wife would sometimes warn me when we were going to a party to watch my words. She would say that while she was fine with my loose choice of expressions, other people found it offensive. But when I asked Epinoia if it's okay to use curse words, she giggled and said nobody in the afterlife cares. She said swearing is a good way to shed the remaining anger from being in a body. When I asked if it would offend God, she burst into a whole-hearted laugh. "You're so funny," she said. "You think you can change God's mind. Oh, sweetheart, God's mind is already made up about you, and everyone else. It's your mind that needs to change. If swearing offends you, then you have an issue with guilt, which is what keeps you trapped in hell. The opposite of hell is forgiveness, so let's forgive the terrible words you're about to say. It's not God's forgiveness, because God doesn't have anything to forgive. It's your forgiveness for that which never happened."

I gave her another blank look, but she told me I'd eventually know the Love of God, as everyone would, foulmouthed or not.

When I say that I had a blank look, don't get the wrong idea; I no longer have a face. Epinoia told me she doesn't have a face either; nobody does. Neither does God, for that matter. But she had pulled together a form for my sake, to make it easier for me to focus. When I asked her why I needed to focus, she giggled and said, "You'll see. This is a classroom, like being in a body is a type of classroom. To help you focus, we'll use what you think of as bodies. The body isn't real, but it will help us figure stuff out together. It's just easier that way. It's what you're used to."

What I discovered in death, or the afterlife, isn't what I expected at all. A room full of magic mirrors with a giggling angel and the lack of a body wasn't something I would have come up with. Epinoia explained that while I was in my last dream, I'd had a couple of what she called "Holy Instants," tiny moments of opening my mind to be led, rather than trying to lead and control. These tiny moments (and we reexperienced them together, so I knew exactly what she was telling me) had brought me to the point where I asked God for a better way. When she reminded me, I remembered actually saying out loud, "God, there must be a better way. Show me what it is, and I will accept it, without question. Lead, and I will follow." She reminded me that when I allowed God to be God, that's when I was shown the house of mirrors in this afterlife, or death, or what she called the Borderland.

We both giggled together at these remembrances, and I thought, *Borderland. Is this a place, then?* And she said, "Nope, not a place — and not in time, so not a when *when,* either. It's an overlap between Reality and myth." I then asked if this was purgatory, to which she replied, "Oh, heavens, no! Purgatory is an imagined place of suffering, and all suffering is the same. No, this is the Borderland, the formless idea where a waking extension of God starts to accept the Love of God more completely." She went on to tell me not to worry so much about the names of things. "Names are a way that egos try to own and control their experience. What you call 'God' cannot be named or controlled. Simply allow the experience to lead you. You're in a state of mind that is not yet in Heaven, because you are still holding onto fear. But you have evolved enough to come one step closer to Heaven. Well, not really *closer*, because that would imply there is distance to cover, and there isn't. Let's just say your mind is opening up to the knowledge of God, and you are on the brink of letting go of trying to understand God." She giggled. "You'll see ... literally."

Then Epinoia shared with me a moment from my last experience in a body when I had just finished cutting the grass in my backyard and was putting the lawn furniture back in place. At the time, my family and I lived on an inland lake, and when I looked out at the lake, the water was acting strangely. A creek was trickling in one direction while the wind was pushing the water in another direction, and the pattern was absolutely mesmerizing. At that moment, my ego slipped away from my consciousness, and in an instant, this lovely feeling of oneness came over me. I was no longer a person in a body, and what I witnessed was a momentary glimpse into the Mind of God. The experience was a memory wrapped in timelessness, covered in the silk of Love, and surrounded by the music of God's own voice. All the birds were singing just for me. All the flowers were blossoming just for me. The water, trees, grass, and stones were all alive, and an extension of my own imagination. I was no longer a person living in separation; I was One with God. If you know what I'm describing, you have experienced it, too. If not, you actually have experienced it; you've just forgotten and will one day remember that original experience.

Then Epinoia giggled and said, "One of your moments of forgiveness, and an expansion of God. Pretty cool, wouldn't you agree? That's why you're imagining being in a room full of magic mirrors. This is your imagination trying to explain life in a body, and to come to terms with the illusion of being a body. You are taking responsibility for everything you have experienced. Spirit is telling you that you were never a body; you've always been free. The prison of a body was something you made up out of fear, and you are just awakening from that fear. You still need a moment, but you'll get there. Everyone does eventually, no matter what they think they've experienced. All these mirrors you see? It's all you, baby! Time after time, life after life, all of it insane — and none of it real." Then she giggled again and asked me to walk with her, which was funny because, you know, I didn't have a body at the moment. So, I drifted along.

Chapter 2.

Where to Start?

I asked Epinoia, "Why are we born into bodies, then? Didn't God create us as bodies?"

That's not a question, as it turns out. Neither is wondering why we *think* we are people in bodies (and I thought I was clever to come up with that). These are statements. Epinoia explained, "When we ask, 'Why am I here?' or 'Why do we think we're here?', we are saying we are someplace else, or we are in a place that isn't where our spirit belongs, or we are in a body, in a situation, doing stuff — working, having babies, having fights, talking to people, making love, eating, making art, engaging in science, and on and on. All that meaningless *doing* stuff. We are also saying we are a separate being, in a body, on a planet, living a life. So many extensions of God have this question that it needs to be answered. To that, I offer the following — but keep in mind, it's all metaphorical. None of this is in fact 'true.' Only God is true. The rest of us are just making all this stuff up."

This is what she told me:

"In the perfect whiteness, there is awareness, which is an extension of the One who has thought everything into existence. Doing what It does, creating like Itself, It extends Love into Being where there was nothing before. From the white void springs sentience, as a reflection of the Perfection that created it.

"Imagined into being, the One reflected back on Itself and was aware that It had been thought and reflected the thought with original Love that was everything. The One who had Created and the one who had been created were of the same mind, the same will, and like each other in every respect. Both creative, the Creator and created were in the same mind, in every way identical, save for one: that One created the other like Itself without separation, sharing one will in every way.

"Then in an instant, a decision was made to break wills with the Creative, and in that moment, with the seriousness of a Southern minister, its reflection reached for a desire to be separate, to have its own will, as distinguished from that of the Creative. A joke without a punch line, a suicide of wills that created *dual* and *duel* in a single thought.

"Then the white void from which awareness dawned was shattered into tiny bits that streamed out across space and made-up time. Darkness suddenly surrounded the tiny remnants, like distant stars, reminders that what once was One is now many — too many to be counted, or even accounted for. The created scattered into cold darkness, as vast as the Love was deep and warm. Infinitesimal streams of awareness splattered throughout space and came to hide in the corners of the Creative mind as tiny extensions of light, chased by the delusion of guilt. At that moment, a giant metaphorical broken dryer started to vibrate, creating noise to cover up the trail, obscuring the path back to the Source by fabricating the illusion of time and space.

"In that unholy instant, a decision for suicide was made that would birth the idea of time and space, scattering the whiteness into a swath of beige, subject to the whims of nature, casting itself out naked to fend for itself. It is a decision that must be made time and time again to maintain the fantasy, a struggle to try to balance the Creative with personal identity, a desire to walk back into the Creative and be recognized as a separate creative entity. This is a dream of youthful folly — a dream that is perpetuated on countless planets, in countless galaxies, by countless sentient beings, all with the desire to be recognized by the

Creative as whom they see themselves to be, and pointing to all the others as different and somehow less worthy of God's attention and recognition.

"Like screaming children demanding that the Creative be the way they deem It should be, it is a tantrum of spiritual immaturity, operating under the misguided impression that if there are enough like minds and every disparate mind is winnowed out, like weeds that can be pulled until the lawn of creativity looks like one vast sea of uniformity, then the Creative will stand up and notice and give recognition where it is long overdue.

"See me, yet don't see me; I'm fearless, yet fearful; I seek, but do not find. And the metaphorical dryer goes on getting louder and looks for signs that point away from the truth, rather than towards it. Hiding out and longing to be found, and all the while, God does what God has always done: God creates like unto Itself in Its own image. Love creates only Love, and that which is not Love makes up only myths.

"You, my dear, have unplugged the giant broken dryer to reclaim the precious silence and are just now learning who you are in reality. You have come to a state of mind in which you are no longer screaming, and you are working through your guilt. You have come to God's Loving Peace, and because you are taking responsibility for all you have encountered in your dreams, you are ready to have God take the final step towards you."

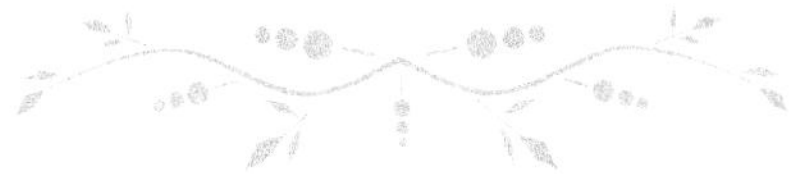

My focus turned back to the magic mirrors with a sudden understanding. The darkness of the entire ego dream came down on me, and I could feel the fear, anger, guilt, and shame of every entity that had ever lived on any planet, in any galaxy. The seething mix of feelings was overwhelming. The loneliness was a feeling of homelessness, without any memory of where home could be, lost without any sense of direction. Like a marble on an uneven table, my mind was rolling off the edge of awareness, until Epinoia caught me with a glimmer of love, gently pulling me back into the embrace of Holiness.

Epinoia said, "Yes, like I said before, every mirror is you. An infinite number of dreams. All the so-called "good people," and all the so-called "bad people." The dreams of you as rich and famous beyond belief, and the dreams of your poor, murderous, and self-loathed personalities. Every magic mirror you see here reflects *you*. Your mind made it all up, as far as you can see and beyond, each playing itself out over and over again, like a broken record."

She continued, "Let's take a journey together and find forgiveness for each dream."

My initial thought was that it would take forever to get through all these experiences. *There are so many dreams here, I simply can't imagine having to...*

She cut through my worries. "When you find forgiveness for some of these dreams, many of the others will fall like dominos. What you do in the now can have an effect on the past and the future. This is because there isn't any time; there is only now. We start where your intuition leads you to start. You're ready for this. Allow the Holiness that is who you are to draw you to a starting point, and go from there. I'll be here with you to keep you from slipping back into your ego mind. In reality, we have always been with you from the start. When you became aware, that awareness was overwhelming, and you fainted. A deep sleep came over you, and your mind started to make up stories as a way of hiding from the Love of God. That sounds counterintuitive, but the Truth of God is very powerful, and you didn't accept that you are Holy. When you fell into the deep sleep, God whispered into your mind the answer to your mistaken belief that you are not worthy of God's Love. That whisper is me." And then she giggled.

She could see I was hesitant, and she added, "Travel with me and realize the truth about time and space: time is projected, and space is brought near. There is a distance we would keep between each of us, and this space is perceived as time. This makes trust impossible between the two of us, and all of humanity."

For a moment, my mind went blank, and my awareness wasn't clear or precise. Does that make sense? Consciousness elapsed. Epinoia's voice became distant and echoing, like she had fallen down a tunnel. If I still had eyes, I would have cried like a lost child at a carnival with no hope of ever being found.

Epinoia called me back. "Blip! Stay with me, my love." She giggled. "Can you look beyond the illusion? We shall see, won't we? Now, do you remember many lifetimes ago, when you said you never wanted to go through any of this again? You had once been king of a tribe on a mountain, but all your family was taken from you. You were then enslaved and forced to dig for precious metals for your captors, and you eventually died of exhaustion. You said, 'God, I hate you! Never do this to me again. All I ever did was what you told me to do, and this is how you thank me.' Do you remember?"

Images of that planet, of that time, of my wife and children started to come to me — vague flashes of faces, moments, and landscapes, but nothing I could hold onto.

"Ah, there we go; your intuition is starting to draw you in. Do you trust God? Do you trust me? Do you trust yourself? At this moment, the answer is no. You still trust the ego, which is not worthy of your trust. But in one Holy instant, that will change. What we are going to do is look beyond the insanity of the illusion and see all your brothers and sisters as sinless. We're going to look at each moment and realize there isn't truly good or bad, right or wrong, or anything for us to judge. Everything you see, it's all an illusion. All the mirrors are the same. They may seem to reflect different forms, but the problem, the answer, and the healing are all the same."

More images of that life flashed into my mind, when I was king and then conquered, and my wife and children were all raped and enslaved. Yellow, dust, black hair, and pearly eyes. Thick, rich, glistening metal. And pain. Deep, deep sadness.

"As the images come to you, as you look into each mirror, realize your judgment isn't correct, because you do not have the knowledge to judge correctly. You simply cannot judge, even though you do it anyway. Ego justice is never true justice. It is always vengeful and punishing. Each mirror you perceive is a judgment — not made by God, but by you, your ego. God has already judged all of this to be a lie, and each of these illusions is an argument you are having with God. Only God's Truth is True, nothing else, and the argument is one-sided. You argue, and God waits patiently for you to let go of your argument."

Temples, sharp edges, a deep blue sky, a dry, warm sun, bronzed male bodies in chains, women raped and beaten. Laughing faces, spitting faces, preachers shouting that we are all heathens and deserve what we're experiencing.

"My beloved, you are fearful to see. You do not trust what you think God will show you. But these are not images of

God. God offers only Love and Happiness, which are one and the same. You, you, you. Me, me, me. The idea keeps us separate, but we are one. One mind: God's mind. When the world would become fuzzy around the edges and the light would come through, you would turn away in fear. You thought your mind, the ego mind, was slipping from you. Your ego told you the loss would be too great. The sacrifice that you were convinced God was asking of you was more than you could bear."

Seemingly endless days of torture and pain. Hot, blistering sun. Cold, piercing nights. Thirsty, always thirsty, and hungry, never enough food.

"But together, we will begin to understand cause and effect. The effect is the mirror. The cause is a lack of trust in the Holy Spirit. One tiny, crazy idea that you could be separate from God, and from your brothers and sisters, has created a near infinity of magic mirrors, and pain and suffering that seems to go on for all eternity."

Realigning with the insanity of that ancient time, my mind slipped into a mirror.

"The first real question for you to answer is, can you buy your innocence with someone else's guilt? In this mirror of this ancient planet, your innocence is based on another's guilt. It's impossible to get to what you call Heaven when you see other people as bad and yourself as good, or the other way around. When you ask God to compare you to them, God can't do that. Not because God is weak or stupid, but simply because God cannot make what is false True. Only the Truth is True."

Chapter 3.

A King, Another King, and Yet More Kings

In an instant, I slipped more completely into one of the robed bodies, and the magic mirror absorbed my memory of an imagined experience on a distant planet, where I envisioned a life with my people at the top of a mountain. Everything was stone — our homes, markets, and temples, all made of sun-drenched stone. The space was an oasis in an otherwise dusty desert. My tribe was olive-skinned and black-haired with pearly brown eyes. The cities were chiseled into geometric shapes, buildings carved from stone, adorned with lovely plants that brought color and shade to an otherwise monochromatic environment. I remembered that I had a large family with both sons and daughters, and a wife, whom I remembered as very lovely. She was slender, with a delicate voice and striking eyes, and I reminisced that I loved to hear her laugh. She was terrific with our children, and even better with me. The impression was one of complete peacefulness. What I dreamed might as well be the perfect life in a body.

My loving people on the mountaintop lived well. We would spend countless hours laughing, playing, singing, and eating at banquets. What we didn't know was that we were living on a mountain of valuable metal. Like gold, this metal was buttery and pliable, but unlike gold, once the metal was smelted and formed, its color, mostly a deep yellow, would change with the light. In the early mornings it would look purple, then become warmer until about midday, when it would be its natural rich yellow, and finally it would turn red throughout sunset and become a deep blue-green at night. Our tribe used it for decoration, but not much else. It wasn't worth anything to us other than for its natural beauty.

We never thought much about the metal, until a group of people we had never seen before visited us and told us we were not using the metal correctly. They said the metal could be made into coins and used to create wealth. They told us all we were doing was making art with it and sitting around laughing. They told us we should work to get the metal out of the mountain, so we could be rich and live a life of ease. When we told them it seemed to us that we were already doing just that, they came at us with hatred and threats of war and called us "stupid" and "heathen." They said we were savages and didn't understand the laws of money or value, and that if we didn't give them the metal we were living on, they would take it by force.

We laughed at first, because there was just a handful of these people. Our tribe was large and healthy, and we could easily defend ourselves, if it came to that. Finally, these other people left us, and for many years we didn't think much about them. We continued to live our lives and decorate with the so-called "precious metal." But one day, they returned with many men, all equipped for war. They overtook our small outer cities and tortured and beat the inhabitants to death. They killed the women and children and enslaved the men to do labor for them. Over time, I witnessed the angry foreign army overtaking my tribe, raping and pillaging everything in sight. Once they had conquered our tribe, the men brought in other men dressed in robes and bearing books, and they forced us to learn the ways of their god, whom they said would not tolerate our heathen religious practices. They told us theirs was the one true god, who was angry with us, and that if our mythical gods had been the true gods, we would have won the war and our tribe would have survived.

These fearful people called our tribe "savages." They said we were cruel and vicious and aggressively hostile. We barely fought back, and yet we were called savage. I watched with tear-filled eyes as one after another fucked my wife and daughters in front of me, then sold them all into slavery. Yet *I* was the savage heathen who needed to be taught the ways of their god.

In that life, I carried the greed and desires of other men for a couple decades. I was forced to dig into my mountain home, where my family had lived and grown for many thousands of years. I pulled wagons filled with that so-called precious metal over the bloodstains of my kin, being beaten for not working fast enough, and starved because I was deemed unworthy of being fed. Finally, I died a slow and agonizing death, a slave to these insane men with power and fear in their hearts. Gradually, my body was drained of all its energy until my heart simply stopped beating.

For what seemed like a millennium, I suffered, lost in a crazy dream, caught in a nightmare. But like a distant call or the sweetness of a gentle song came the voice of recognition. It was Epinoia reaching out to me. Her voice was clear, where my dusty dream in the desert was slightly out of focus. If you've ever worn glasses or contacts for the first time, or had eye surgery, you'll understand what I'm describing. She was a whisper at first, but then she became all I was listening to.

"My beloved, here you are, one of the good people. Yet your innocence is dependent on the guilt of those 'bad people' — a comparison you draw so that God will see you and recognize just how much better you are than them. You see this life as a sacrifice. But my beloved, in this dream, as in every dream, you are everyone. You are the colonel who raped your wife and beat you into submission, driven by your own desire to control and dominate. You are your wife, raped, helpless, naked, a slave to the lust of human desire. You are also the rapist, as much a slave to lust as your wife was to helplessness. You are your children, all sold off like chattel. Like pieces in a puzzle, they all fit together perfectly, because they are all in your mind. It is all your own dream."

She continued, "The forgiveness you offer is not for the colonel, or your wife, or your people, or your children. And your forgiveness is not offered as a gift to absolve someone lesser than you in mind or spirit. The forgiveness is for yourself. The dream is yours, my dear, precious child."

I followed her voice, and it grew clearer. I became more peaceful, and my mind became quiet. In the quietness of my mind, Epinoia's voice was like a gentle summer rain on the parched earth of my desert dream. She continued, "You see, my love, you want so much to think you would never do any of those things. You want with all your being to place blame on someone else, to say, 'They did this, and they did that, and look how they behaved! I would never ever in a million years do any of that to anyone, ever.' And you want God to punish them, to make sure they can never get away with any of that behavior again. This is an attempt to use guilt as a free pass to enter Heaven."

Fear then turned into anger; I did indeed want the colonel and all his evil men to rot in hell. I wanted them to die and stand before a god of judgment, who would laugh at them as they became weak, naked, and helpless. More than that, I wanted that god to wave his hand and send them off to live in hell for all eternity, and even that would not be enough to make me happy. The feeling was raw and hateful.

Epinoia was correct. I didn't want to offer forgiveness, nor to take responsibility; I wanted revenge. My happiness was thus linked to their guilt and suffering. I was trying to buy my way into Heaven on the backs of other people's guilt. I, the good person, should get to go to Heaven alone, and they, those others, the bad people, should perish in hell and rot for all eternity. As long as I held onto that thought — my own idea of good and evil — the mirror of the desert pain would stand strong.

Epinoia said, "But you know if they are in prison, so are you. Love can never be bought with guilt. Your freedom is in your mind. You're not forgiving them; you are forgiving yourself. Let your mind open to God's Loving Reality. Quiet your mind and see all this differently. Hanging onto your anger and hatred will only bring you more of the same. Only forgiveness can save you. Open your mind, my beloved, and allow God to take that final step towards you. God can only do that if you are willing. It is now and has always been your choice."

When she said this, I felt my mind slipping into the colonel's body. Hatred filled my spirit, but underneath the hatred was fear and resentment. However misplaced, these feelings were directed towards a group of brown-skinned, dark-eyed people whose metal I wanted. What I thought of as my former self limped by, and the hatred grew deeper. Nothing was clearer in my mind at that moment than my desire to crush the weakness of a so-called king who would give up his land and possessions so easily. I was a dark-haired, crippled, and defeated shadow of a once powerful being that now had nothing left to live for, yet still I hobbled around, scraping bits of metal from the ground.

My thoughts at that moment became filled with desire: for metal, for power, for control, and to hide from the call of death. As a colonel, I was trying to reach ever higher in the eyes of those I respected. My king, my troops, and anyone I cared to impress were all that mattered, and I assumed they all thought the way I did. Having a dark-skinned king's wife wait on me, half naked, crying herself to sleep gave me a feeling of absolute power. To those I conquered, I was a god, and they were pathetic, weak, and worthless. I held in my hands the power of life and death, and nobody could disobey me.

But beneath that feeling of power was the knowledge that everything I held onto was ephemeral. Nothing we were digging out of the earth would ever be enough. I was a hungry, pale ghost, searching for the Love of God, but not having a clue as to where to find it. So, I searched and sought, but nothing filled the emptiness in my soul. As with a fishnet trying to hold water, my desires would dribble out the moment I lifted my mind. The accusations in the black eyes of the dark-skinned people I had enslaved were spat back at me. I had won, and in that moment, even though the moment was but a simple flash of lightning against the cumulonimbus clouds of eternity, I was more powerful than kings.

As the colonel, I became encapsulated in my own feelings of superiority. Nothing could stop me. I even went so far as to skim off some of the precious metal to build my own wealth. I would later get caught by the king who had sent me to conquer the foreign land, and be hanged as an example, to prove that there was only one king. As in a spiderweb, we were all caught up in the insane belief that anything that was happening was real. The king who hung me would eventually die himself, and on and on the echoes of hatred and fear would ripple out — until Epinoia called me back.

As my mind became quiet, she said, "Free will is choosing to align your will with God's Will. That will *is* the extension of Love. You were king, then king, then king, and king yet again — and it got you nothing. Each time you thought you had reached the top, you could only hold on for a moment or two, and then, *poof*, gone! Only God's Love is eternal. Only God's extension of Love is worth searching for. And it has always been here, waiting for you. Funny, huh? Makes you wanna giggle, doesn't it?

"That's all for now, my beloved." And then she did giggle.

At that moment, I came back to the house of magic mirrors, some of which had disappeared. There were plenty of mirrors still standing, but some of them were in fact gone. I found my mind quiet and peaceful, and I was a bit surprised at how many mirrors had vanished just from that one experience. The egos of the colonel, the kings, and my family had evaporated, and in that moment, I could no longer remember anything other than the Perfect God Love we had shared in those so-called lifetimes.

Chapter 4.

A Faraway Planet

Because time doesn't exist, and because I was in the Borderland, the feeling of bliss may have gone on for an eternity, and at the same time, maybe for just a moment or two. Funny thing about not being attached to a body, on a planet, living what we call a life: time isn't obvious. What ultimately brought me back or captured my attention in the Borderland of mirrors were flashes of light. Imagine a meteor shower, but more like a heavy rain, with streaks of light flowing down like a waterfall. My attention was drawn to one tiny sliver of light, and as I slipped into another body, the magic mirror sprang to life.

Epinoia said, "Time is not linear. Truth be told, time doesn't exist at all in the Mind of God. But I'm helping you relive the story of an ego, and so, that story must be told in time and space. It looks like you're ready for another lesson in forgiveness and understanding."

Epinoia started to fade again, and her voice became a distant echo as I imagined a place many light-years from anywhere I had been before, in a time long past and mostly forgotten, when there was a planet not unlike Earth. A fearful people had tried to tame their planet and enslave each other, and at the same time, they claimed to have attained freedom. They had prisons, but mostly the people were free. As on Earth, people in some places could come and go as they pleased, and spaces were offered for the owners of most everything to go and plan and live, while other places on the planet served to support their elaborate plans and lifestyles. While some people had several homes, all the support people — the background people — lived at the mercy of those who owned everything. Yet nearly everyone thought their salvation depended on this complex network of relationships.

Epinoia commented, "Your mind is split in this dream. You are of two minds: the True mind, that which is in alignment with God-Love, and the other mind, that which is in alignment with the insanity of the material world, the world of bodies and things — coins, clothing, houses, automobiles, and expressions of egoic passions and desires.

The sliver of light you followed is a memory of this split mind. When you think of freedom in this nightmare, the ego mind associates this with bodies. Yet freedom is a mental state, a state of mind. Alone in a prison, or alone in a crowd, it matters not. All bodies are prisons, and all ego experiences are suicidal. What you experience as life in a body was never truly created, only made up. It is God's Mind twisted out of proportion, held together for a brief moment, and then it disbands."

The people of this faraway planet had become very good at justifying their behavior and lifestyles, so when the planet started to falter, they had great debates about what to do to preserve their planet and save themselves. Some insisted the signs indicated that everyone on the planet would soon die unless substantial changes were made; others said no, the planet was very strong, and the people who lived there were not doing anything to truly harm their home. But for the most part, the people didn't take any action, because they thought themselves too small and insignificant to do anything to save an entire planet. And the great landlords didn't want any changes that might cause them to lose their imagined power, so they would have none of the talk about the planet being in peril and declared it unpatriotic to speak of such things.

Maybe I thought the same thing. Maybe I believed that my salvation depended on the complex set of circumstances we had built as a society. I don't recall whether I owned a lot or anything, but I do remember the end. I was born late in the life cycle of the civilization of that planet, so I remember the arguments and sarcasm, the fights and wars, and the constant justifications for our behavior. I especially remember the final days, when the priests told us to repent because the end was near. Not that it was difficult to predict; as I recall, everything had become chaotic. Turbulent weather tore through our cities, people went on killing sprees, and those wanting more control called for stiffer penalties and harsher, more outrageous regulations on other people.

Epinoia's voice became clearer. "Maybe you thought the same thing? Maybe you thought all of this? It is your dream — one that a simple change of mind can cure. But I'll let you experience it the way you imagined it, and we can find forgiveness once you get it all out."

In my imagination, none of what we tried as a society had worked. Ultimately, we were not willing to set aside our fears and do what was necessary to find peace. But what we didn't realize was that the planet was only a reflection of what was in our hearts. Some thought God was punishing us, and they cast the responsibility on people who didn't live a certain way. "If only those other people would behave. If only they/them/those others could just get past their lust and wanton desires, we would all be at peace." Others blamed the wealthy oligarchs and their lust for money and power;

it was all their fault. In the end, we were all trying hard to use guilt and shame to buy our way into Heaven.

When the planet failed, it happened quickly and violently — or at least it seemed that way to me. Just a few years, and then a chain reaction of events occurred, and it was over. I remember souls streaming off the planet, like slivers of light pouring out in all directions. Looking back on it, I can still remember thinking how beautiful it was, the silver light like billions of shooting stars cascading like a sparkling fountain and then spreading to the corners of the known and unknown universes.

The moment of understanding came to me when I looked back on the planet and watched all my spirit brothers and sisters spring from the surface in great waves like silver lines, each perfect and exactly the same. Where we had been separate, now we were all one, and then separate again. But in that instant, the memory of the God-Love feeling washed over me, and I suddenly realized we were all an extension of God. Not one sliver of light was any different from the next. They were not the same in a military or industrial way, but in a way that showed God's Work in Its purist sense. It was there for just an instant — or perhaps forever — and then as suddenly as the feeling had come over me, I felt the tug of my ego calling me back. And the moment I tried to put words to the God-Love memory, it was gone. It was as though my ego pushed it away.

I share this story to bring you comfort. The end of your Earth is near, but it is not the end of anything, in reality. What does the end of an illusion look like? We are not truly bodies being hurled around a star. That doesn't mean we shouldn't act as stewards of our home, but it does mean that our own awakening doesn't depend on this one planet in this one galaxy.

As I remembered this ancient experience on a distant planet, a deep feeling of nostalgia washed over me. But that's too easily overlooked; the feeling was deeper. Do you remember being a child on your first trip away from home and getting homesick? No, that's not right, either. Imagine someone close to you dies, someone you love with very few complaints or exceptions. They die unexpectedly — like me getting hit by a bus. They start to fade from your memory, and with those memories, your ability to remember what they looked like, sounded like, and everything about them fades as well. No matter how hard you try to hang onto those wonderful thoughts, they slip away from you, leaving a hole in your heart that can never be filled. So, you beg to die and go to Heaven, where you can be together, but at the same time, you have this sinking feeling that it will never happen. You worry that they are forgetting you as well. But this is all happening because you think you are a separate person — two people separated by a sudden death, which seems permanent. You know, until you remember this on your own, there simply isn't any way to explain the feeling, except to say that you know this feeling as well as you know the feeling of God-Love. We all do. It is in the very foundation of who we are.

While I watched all those little slivers of light shoot off like comets, I felt like we were making a mistake, leaving our world behind like that. Then the idea came to me that we would just keep finding, civilizing, and then killing new planets over and over again, like a gerbil on a wheel, running and running, but never getting anywhere. I also felt that I was running away from God — that God was after me. Me shooting off like a star was my way of searching for hiding places where God would never even think of looking.

Epinoia said, "You can't miss anyone. But that isn't to say what you think you felt isn't what you felt. It is just to say that when you accept your place in Heaven, every loving memory is already there in Heaven with you. Baby, there is no other. It's just you, sweet pea. What you're longing for is the Love of God, and that's already yours. That's what you are looking for. That is what everyone is looking for."

My attention was drawn to the feeling of God chasing me, being angry with me.

"My beloved, God doesn't chase anyone. You are an extension of God. God made you in Its own image, like Itself, and that idea will never leave Its source. God created You with Love in Its own image. You are worthy of that Love because God has decided that it is so. You have never truly civilized a planet, yet you have seemingly experienced the end of countless planets in countless universes. When you're in a body, can your left hand hide from your right hand? You are a part of God; God is You. God's Mind is your mind. God wills you to have everything It has to offer, and instead, you make planets and search where God can never be found. You do not ask for too much, my beloved; you ask for far too little. You ask for a moment in time, rather than the Love of All Time."

The slivers of light became a space of pure white light, and Epinoia said, "My sweet child, God doesn't need to forgive you. God isn't angry with you, no matter what you think you have done, or said, or not done. You need to let go of your dreams of insanity. Correcting the dreams is not up to you. You go from one dream to another, looking to 'get it right this time.' But that's not your function. That function belongs to God, Who knows of fairness, not of guilt. Guilt will not get you into Heaven. Guilt and shame will keep you from Heaven. Look at your story. It's all about accusations. But you cannot forgive until you learn that fixing what's wrong is not your role, and looking for fault is not your role, either. Stop accusing and realize that it is forgiveness that will lead to correction, as they are one and the same."

I started to say, "But they — "

"But they, them, those others — they are sinners. They need to be punished. Me and mine are all just mistakes that need to be corrected and forgiven — but those others, they deserve punishment.' That's never going to get you where you want to go, my dearly beloved. When you understand that correcting mistakes and pardoning that which you perceive has happened, but never has, are the same, you will also understand that your mind and the Holy Spirit's Mind are the same."

With that statement, my mind was drawn back to Epinoia. I had been looking at her as someone separate from me. I have a mind; she has a mind; the people I knew and hated and the people I knew and loved all had minds of their own. And then there was God's Mind, which was simply awesome — a Mind I could never know and was not worthy of knowing. God would always be out of reach, from the perspective of my ego.

Maybe I wasn't ready for this truth. Perhaps I was simply not far enough along in my awakening to accept what she had just said.

Epinoia replied, "No, you *were* ready, or you would not have heard me. But you could always hear me, just as you can always hear God. You can always be in Heaven. It is your mind that must change, not God's Mind. God's Mind is perfect, stable, and you cannot change God's Mind about anything. These lessons are not for God. They are for you, my beloved." And then she giggled.

She continued, "I am not a messenger from hell, sent by God to wreak vengeance. But my love is not something that a 'sinner' can understand. This is because they think love is split off from justice, so all they know is vengeance. Quiet your mind, and in that quietness, you will find the mercy that God offers. Realize that love and justice are not different. Because they are the same — justice and love combined as one — the mercy of God is offered to every mind that has ever been, and in that knowledge is the power to forgive yourself, my beloved. I don't know how else to put this, but the mind you think you have is truly an extension of God's Mind. Everything we think we think is in God's Mind."

My attention was drawn inward — not into a body, but to my mind. Of course, when I say "inward," there isn't really any inside or outside, so don't take me literally. What happened was that I fell deeply into quietness, like an infinite pond of cool, clear water on a summer day, with no breeze to cause even the smallest ripple on its surface. In that depth of awareness, I came to the knowledge that God's justice cannot punish anyone, even those who ask for punishment, because God is a Judge Who knows what God created is wholly innocent in Truth. There is great comfort in knowing I had been wrong about everything.

As this knowledge came to me, something else happened: the idea of being someone, a personality, slipped away from me completely. What I was left with was a remembrance of perfect Love. When I tell you this, think of it as a memory so perfect and loving that it is still fresh and new. But it was an experience that I recognized. Know that you have had this experience as well. You may not think so now, in this moment, but I assure you that for me, there was nothing about this experience that was special.

A gentle voice entered my awareness and said, "The true meaning of peace is very simple: nothing God created can ever truly be harmed. In essence, nothing that can be harmed is real."

I sat with that in the meantime, long enough for the peacefulness of the idea to saturate my entire awareness. All the lives — the pain, sorrow, fear, and guilt I had experienced — were simply not real, and they faded away into a cold, dark void. Nothing ephemeral is real. If it was born and it dies, it is not of God, and therefore it is not of anything.

The darkness was all around me; my mind was being drawn into a void. So, I called to Epinoia for guidance. I felt worn out, tired, exhausted.

She said, "You can be weary, but not tired. You don't have a body, and tiredness is an expression of the body. Together, we're making excellent progress. The darkness you are experiencing all around you is another lesson you're ready to forgive. Let's take another step. And remember, we are here for you, my beloved."

And then she giggled.

Chapter 5.

My First Trip to Earth

I came to a mirror of a time on Earth in what would be called the Dark Ages in human history. My memory of this lifetime was sketchy at first, which isn't surprising. It's hard enough to remember the recent past, much less the past several lifetimes. But the fact that I can't remember each moment of every life isn't a great deficit, as it turns out. I once thought so. I harbored a fear that the day after my body died, I would find myself on a beach somewhere, perhaps in purgatory, and Jesus, sitting in a lounge chair, would look over at me and say, without any sense of irony, "Jeez, what was that all about?", and my inability to remember a significant detail of some life experience that was related in an important way to that final question would result in an entire afterlife of pain and misery.

Of course, I now know that's not at all true. What I know now is that what I'm looking for — what we are all looking for — is not to be found in some detail or equation. It's not even a word or phrase, or a prayer or book of any kind. I now realize that what we're looking for cannot be found in any myth, whether religious or scientific, because there are no true stories of God, or equations in science that will explain God, but only a remembering of the gift that God has given us. And that is simply all that is real: that part of anyone that wasn't born and never dies. So, as we look around us and think about how we got here and why, we fail to realize that we do all that thinking in a borrowed mind.

Epinoia said, "Once there was magic. But magic is always of the ego because it is always of the body. We are not bodies, however, so magic is not real. But magic can be used by the Holy Spirit to bring us to Reality, if we will allow it to."

As I recall in that lifetime, there was magic, but not everyone could see it, or experience it, or express it. But some people who were bereft of magic were powerful in other ways. They had wealth and influence in a primitive civilization, and they had strength in their bodies, cunning in their minds, and a desire to stamp out their fear of magic. So, they schemed and created a dogma they could impose on other people in the hopes of enslaving their fears.

Many people today believe in science, not in magic, and there seems to be a misguided idea that the god of science will reveal all the mysteries of the universe eventually. These people seem to think her mysteries will be coaxed, stolen, and seduced out of nature, the way a boy might cajole a schoolgirl out of her panties, and that humans will at some point be able to harness life itself, controlling every aspect of nature to the point that it serves our will completely. Conversely, there are others who think that God has a vested interest in how our lives are lived and is really angry about how we're doing so far. They believe he (it's always a *he*, isn't it?) has a desire to beat us to death, then banish everyone who doesn't conform to these psychotic whims to unrelenting anguish for all eternity — a psychopathic or sociopathic god who creates creatures with natural desires and proclivities, then condemns them to untold torture unless they deny that very desire in favor of some other pursuit.

It has taken me many lifetimes to awaken to the thought that perhaps the god of hate should accept some responsibility for all the crap he created and doesn't like. Seriously, it is a strange mind that creates someone, then condemns that individual for not being what it wanted in the first place. Imagine breathing life into the soul of a creature of your own design, then saying, "Seriously, Betty, you gay freak! I had no idea you would use your free will to have sex with Susie, and for that, I condemn you not to oblivion, oh, no, but to a life of everlasting torture by the hands of some little shit called Satan with a red suit and a pitchfork. And by the way, certain words I find particularly offensive, so if you continue to use them, I'll find a special place in hell for you." That's dramatic, but only to make the point that God would not create a being, offer it free will, and then get angry because that being didn't like what he liked.

Epinoia said, "My beloved, God's mind cannot be changed. If it could, God would be weak and would be subject to death. But as myths go, the god of hate is probably the most difficult. It's also the most destructive. You lay your insecurities and fears at the feet of God, so you can push your guilt off onto someone else. Magic of any kind is a myth, and that includes any story of a god who can change its mind.

"Your anger is misplaced. None of what you are remembering here is of the God of Love. It is all of your own making. This image of an angry God is being created in the ego's image, and it is simply backwards. You, my precious child, need to forgive God. That may sound funny because forgiveness is often misunderstood. When I tell you to forgive God, it may be assumed I think God did something wrong. That is not what I'm referring to here. What I mean is that you must forgive God for that which God never did. It is the true meaning of forgiveness. Not that you are superior, but that you were mistaken in your judgment, and you now realize that this judgment was never up to you in the first place. It is an acknowledgement that your role is not one of judgment."

Epinoia continued, "Some myths are easier to understand than others, depending on your state of mind. In this lifetime, for you, that was the case. But there is no hierarchy of myths; one is not better than another. They are all the same. Now, allow yourself to reach deeply into your mind and experience the moments of these dark times."

I quieted my mind and thought back, and as I did, I remembered being part of a small group, and never having been outside of a few square miles in a forest. While I lived there, I didn't see the changes that were storming towards me like some huge, two-headed monster hell-bent on tearing my brain into little pieces and serving it back to me like coagulated bits of blood sausage. My world at the time was not complicated. We served the many faces of God, all of which were centered on the Great Mother, the giver of all life. The role of men was to serve her, and the role of women was to emulate her. She would give life, and we would tend to that life, as stewards, not as masters. I understood this myth much better than I understood the myths of my other life experiences.

The new religion, this myth that stretches from a few thousand years ago to today — the one that entered my village on horseback with banners and flags and was forced down my throat and held in place like a sweat-soaked gag; the one that killed the feminine face of God and replaced our myth with a new myth of insanity; the one I would struggle with through many centuries and even try on myself as a Bible-thumping, hell-and-damnation minister at one point — has never been the easiest or most logical of pills to swallow. Except in its most mystical form, this new religion that was thrust on me — at sword point at first, and then at gunpoint in other lives — has little or no resemblance to God's True Nature, nor to Its desire for Its Creations. On the mystical side — where gnosis resides, where few of religious nature seem to find their way, and on the very opposite side of the same religious coin that carries a message of fear — there is love, like a flower pressing though rocks and smiling up at the heavens.

Digging in the earth and tending the garden, we came to understand the world contained few things that were not connected to the seeds of life. There was no denying our role. If we didn't tend the garden, the winter would be long and hard, and there was a very good chance we would not live to see the next spring, except for what we might steal from a hibernating squirrel, and frustration might spring from nature's seemingly unkind and unrelenting challenges. We were tied to the earth, and she never let us forget that. When drought came, many suffered and died. What we never realized is how much our thoughts, our wills, had to do with the way the planet behaves. We still don't understand that; even today, we have everything to do with what we witness on the outside, which reflects a direct interdependence with what we have going on in our minds.

My life then was truly simple and fulfilling before the invasion of a projected god. I remember knowing the cycles of the earth. I knew the plants, animals, and weather. I knew the magic that was everywhere, before science crushed and enslaved it. Magic was then tethered in the minds of a few unimaginative souls who might not have even been human, harnessing the energy of nature and making it little, making it their own, and placing a toll on it, then telling everyone that progress can never be made in this world unless there is a chance to enslave others — even to the point of writing in the Bible that obedience as a slave is a doctrine of the almighty: "Slaves, in reverent fear of God, submit yourselves to your masters, not only to those who are good and considerate, but also to those who are harsh" (1 Peter 2:18).

What I understood in that life was when God speaks the way you want God to speak — when he hates the same people you hate and wants the same things you want — you can bet God isn't involved at all. God is never in conflict. God doesn't own property. God doesn't make rules and laws that men obey. It creates only Love. Everything It creates is given all, and what God makes is shared by all and grows through being shared. There is no zero-sum gain. Give it all away, and it doesn't leave. What is given of the god of hate is subtracted. What is given freely of the God of Love grows exponentially. At that time, and even today and well into the future of the ego, the projected god will try to oppress and create poised insanity.

In that dream, I lived in a hut by today's standards, but it was comfortable. It was dug into the earth under a large tree, with thick, smooth walls and small circular windows to let light in. Shutters hung over the windows to provide some control over the light and keep the wind and rain from entering unabated. It contained just a bed, a makeshift table, a chair, and cubbyholes for storage. I was born, lived, and died on one small plot of land, but I was a part of the land and one with everything that lived there with me. I could fly through the brightness of my imagination. I could walk with wolves. I scurried with squirrels and fucked like a bunny. None of us were married, but we paired and formed lifelong bonds.

God was a woman, life-giving and unpredictable, whimsical, loving, and magical, filled to overflowing with emotion and maternal guidance. We respected Her; to do otherwise was to invite a host of misfortunes. The Goddess of all was in balance, and life was tied to Her. When She was angry, our tribe would thin and grow hungry. When She was satisfied, we would grow fat and lazy. We didn't defy Her or try to enslave Her. We understood life was fleeting, and we didn't fear death. We knew that to follow the ego meant we had a finite time in a particular body, but we also knew we would come and go and come again. We were all part of the great mystery that flows through all of physicality.

Days in summer were long, and we hunted, forested, farmed a little, and gathered nuts, berries, and fruit. We knew how to dry and preserve foods. We knew which foods would help with ailments, and we lived in harmony with nature. It was a simple time, and while we spent much of it working, the nights were quiet and warm, and with full bellies, we would talk and dream and perform incantations and pray to the Goddess for guidance and protection.

Fall was my favorite time. The nights would turn brisk, and the air would be clear and crisp. Leaves that had grown would eventually fall gently. The streams would swell with rain, and the night sky would reveal the patterns that would predict the winter. We would plan our harvest accordingly. During the long nights, we would call on our ancestors, whose spirits seemed to spring back to life, their misty bodies translucent, their faces glowing with love and affection. They knew and understood the hardships of winter and would offer us stories that we would tell and retell during the long, cold winter nights when the darkness seemed unending, and even the moon would only peek over the horizon for a few moments every night, then hide away again. Midwinter, the moon would be absent altogether, and it would often feel as though we were lost to the universe.

Warmed by the glow of a fire crackling a constant vigil against the cold, we would huddle together and sleep for long hours, our breathing in rhythm with one another. The women would slowly swell with child over the winter months and produce their fruit in the late spring. A child had the best chance of survival after a long summer of warmth and nourishment, but every so often, a couple would pair too early or too late, and the child would suffer and often die. We didn't look on this as a failure, but instead thought of it as the child making the decision to come at a different time. As with any hardship, we let it flow. Everything in life flows — people, animals, streams, trees, even stones echo the nature of God's Love — and in this way, we never looked at death as a tragedy, but instead as a natural part of the energy that permeates all things, living or dead. We didn't try to conquer death or stuff our feelings. We grieved, and we let the loneliness wash over us in great waves and then pass in their own course. We didn't force our feelings or thoughts out of our minds, and we couldn't busy ourselves to just ignore them. In our tribe, our lives were too slow and relaxed for that nonsense.

Ultimately, our passive nature was our demise. The wicked winds held an unfortunate pattern for what seemed like generations, but even they would eventually change. And while our tribe was small and tired by then, we persevered and recovered. The Great Mother would not destroy our tribe; it was men who would do that. In the name of the unholy church, our ways would be condemned, and our Goddess would be silenced, raped by the god of hate, and relegated to a barren virgin status, serving as little more than a sacred whore.

Fear drove the new religion and enslaved its followers. It allowed men to run with their temper tantrums and slaughter everything in their path. The men in our tribes could also have easily overpowered women and enslaved them. But we didn't enslave women, out of respect for the balance in all things. We listened to women and obeyed their intuitions and their close connection to the Great Mother, Who helped us maintain balance in our society. But it would prove no match for the unrestricted fear and loathing that drove the religion of death and damnation. Like a fierce parasite, it took hold and consumed more gentle societies like ours, proclaiming any passive and gentle society to be backwater, primitive, and subservient.

When religion is turned inside out and projected onto people, it takes on the ugly form of fear. Religion and spirituality are meant to be turned in on ourselves, not out onto others. Only a fool would try to dictate the minds of others, and only a truly disturbed and damaged soul filled with fear would torture others to try to condition them to accept that which is unnatural. God is of light and cannot see the darkness because it is not in Its nature. The Goddess is life-giving and loving, and She paints on a canvas so vast that it is beyond our ability to see or understand intellectually. Only through Love can we begin to understand Her nature. But we were overrun by fools of fear and tormented spirits clothed in shadows, professing worship of a god of death and hatred.

None in our tribe — not even our most advanced priestesses with the highest levels of wisdom — could understand the outward hostility towards women, or the apparent mistrust of the great mysteries of nature. It was foreign to us to look on the world as a thing to be owned and enslaved. To us, the world wasn't a conquest; it was an extension of us, or we were in fact an extension of Her. She had sprung us and supported us and loved us. And while She was not always easy to understand, we loved and respected Her.

Our great leaders went deep into the mists of meditation, and emerged with few answers, most of which drove a wedge into our tribe. Some thought we should leave physical earth for a deeper and truer existence with more enlightened beings. And some among us did move on. They slowed their vibration until they became less and less visible to the rest of the clan. Then, like the passing of clouds, they were gone. I could still connect with them when I was peaceful. They respected our decision to stay but felt deep sadness for our quest for balance in all things, for they knew it would be long and arduous. I think we knew that, too. And perhaps it was folly to pursue a way of life that had been condemned in the name of a false god. While the souls of our clan are few in this realm, and most of them unknown to each other now, some of us are still in your world.

There is a false, Hollywood-style impression of our clan today, portrayed as either barbaric, simple, slow to adjust, and secluded, or shrouded in witchcraft and malice. The image is of little people, dark and mysterious, whom science conquered, or of pointy ears, or large, hairy feet. Always comic, these impressions are also physical and suggest anyone can simply ride a horse to a special tree in the forest during a full moon and slip into a hole and vanish into another long-forgotten world. Stories of devil-worshipers who steal your soul permeate the lost culture, and of the hungry ghosts who move aimlessly through slavery, thinking that they will be the next to take charge of all they see, on a quest to put an end to their fears by killing their enemies and plucking the weeds of society who dare to think deeply or differently.

The truth is much less interesting without a physical frame of reference, but much richer. Our people were beautiful, and yes, some were dark and small, but others were white as ivory. None was more beautiful than another. We never considered one not beautiful, or another more beautiful. We didn't have contests of physical form. Some we wanted to fuck, and that was fine. Others we didn't, but to each his or her own attraction. That isn't to say there wasn't jealously or argument or preferences, but it was balanced with a more feminine perspective. What was beautiful had as much to do with inner beauty as outer. A woman doesn't look at her body parts and measure them unless her power has been stripped from her and all she has left is physical attraction. That was the way of the god of hate. The patriarchy crushed feminine wisdom and perverted it, making it into a pitiful reflection of a male-dominated society. And women were covered and shamed for leading man to Satan and hell. All the blame for sexual energy was cast like a psychological net over women, leaving men to wander in lust without responsibility, and leaving society sexually unbalanced and perverted.

None of our elders or wise-women could fathom the insane idea of this male-dominated society. We could not understand the women who allowed and embraced these perversions, but then, we didn't think on the physical plane, either. We knew we were not our bodies. We knew our nature was spirit, and that while the body is feeble and clumsy, the spirit is graceful. The spirit — that part of you that wasn't born and doesn't die — is just as God created it. Love created like unto Itself and held our pure spirit form in perfect oneness, an inheritance waiting to be reclaimed. This is still as true today as it was back then.

We can still go where many of our tribe chose to reside. The world of light is available to anyone who would align with the vibration of that realm. It's not a place that can be traveled to like on a quest. Many have tried that, but all have failed. Science will tell you it doesn't exist, but then, science will imply that God doesn't exist either, that all spirituality is just so many neurotransmitters in the brain, or a wash of certain neurochemicals, or maybe a tumor or abnormality of some kind. Science is of the body, and the spirit offers no solid evidence. No proof, so, *poof*, it doesn't exist.

But anyone who has slowed down and disconnected from the ego will know that the simplest and most natural state is the one God intended for you, and that science doesn't exist. As if we are groping around in a nightmare, feverishly taking notes, and studying a dream, science can impact the body and convince lost souls that a pill or surgery or certain foods will change everything. But on the spirit level, nothing has changed. Your spirit self, that deep part of you, is still perfect, without the cloud of sin, just the way God thought it into existence. No pills. No imperfection. No guilt.

My end came when I was hung from the very tree that had sheltered me my entire life. There wasn't a trial or any discussion; I was pulled from my little home by a small group of slave owners and told that I was a squatter on their lord's property. They gave me no options — just put a noose around my neck, threw the rope over the thickest part of the tree, and yanked me up. My body was left there until it had decayed beyond recognition. A sign was posted as a warning to anyone of my clan who dared to remain that they would come to the same fate. That I had been born there and lived on that small plot of ground for more than three decades, and that my ancestors had lived there for more than a thousand years held little sway. Strength through the sword was all that mattered, and I didn't have a sword or any inclination to fight back.

It was difficult for me not to hold a grievance. And while I understand God holds no grievances, I did not share Her conviction at the time that those who had hung me deserved forgiveness. It wasn't until Epinoia took the time to explain God's perspective that I began to understand that until I could find forgiveness, without superiority or residual resentment, that these same spiritual situations would occur again and again. The crest for me in this early life was all the peaceful memories of balance, of a life lived in harmony, the simple moments of laughter and love that we felt for each other, the long winter nights wrapped up together in pelts when our breathing synchronized, and we listened to the wind howl and used our imaginations to visit distant places and remember long-lost tribe members. When we slept, we were one, and the God-Love filled our hearts, and then it passed, expelled by our exhales.

Epinoia said, "My beloved, the times of true love and oneness are moments to be remembered. Anything else — the pain and suffering, the attack and murder — those things need to be forgiven and forgotten. None of what happened was real, or of God's desire. God's Will is for perfect happiness. Do you share God's Will for happiness? The life you lived was sometimes happy, and sometimes unhappy. But even the happiest of moments are nothing compared to God's happiness. So much of our so-called lives are illusions of contentment and happiness. But in reality, they are moments of haze, covered in mist, foggy moments of relief. God's Love — that Happiness cannot be expressed in words, nor can it be experienced in a body.

"While your little body was strung up in a tree like a rag doll, other bodies sat and ate lunch, talked, laughed, told stories, and justified their attacks and killing by telling themselves that their lord, the king of all the land, owned the property and everyone on it. They told themselves that their god had given them the right to kill, to cleanse the land of all beliefs that were not in agreement with their own. Their priests and leaders were convinced — just as convinced as you were that your Goddess was the truth — that what they were doing was just, an act of their god on earth.

"Still, all of it was egotistical. One way was not better or more justified than the other. You, my beloved, saw your suffering as payment, as a way to buy your way into Heaven. But that makes no sense. God isn't moved by suffering. God never asked for sacrifice. Furthermore, God didn't ask for a spiritual cleansing, and never asks for an attack of any kind. Attack is simply never justifiable. Killing and attack are never the answer to anything, and God, in Its perfect Love, asks only for Love. When those men hung you from your tree, they were afraid — as fearful as you were. They thought that by killing you, they could waltz into Heaven, and God would look at them and thank them for cleansing the land of the tyranny of the likes of you.

"But God would not thank them. God would wait patiently for them to realize they were doing this out of fear, not Love. Forgiveness would need to come from them, for that which they never did. Then the nightmare that you all share, the one mind that made it all up, would slip into the darkness from which it came and be forgotten. There are no degrees to God's Love. The Love God has for you is exactly the same Love God has for those men who hung you and took your land.

"Are you ready for another idea? There was no 'them'. The dream was yours. The others you thought you experienced were all made up by you. Sit for a while with that thought, my dearest love. Let the knowledge of the Love of God come to you. Accept your place in God's plan and align your will with God's Will."

And then she giggled.

Chapter 6.

A Preacher of Hate

Meditation without a body is different, and so much more enlightening. When I last had a body, my spiritual mentors would tell me to look deep inside myself to find the inner truth that was residing there. I took this to mean going inside myself, as in my body, to look for answers. But the answers were not there. It was like the story my Cub Scout teacher told us when I was a little kid. He did this little play with some of the kids one night in his front yard. His house was on a cul-de-sac and had a streetlamp at the end of the street. It was a fall night, and the sky was already dark in early evening. He asked us to help him look for his keys. Being good little scouts, we all did our best searching under the streetlamp. This went on for about fifteen minutes, until one of the kids asked where he had last seen his keys. He said, "Oh, good question! I last had them up by the garage on the other side of the house." When one of the kids asked why we were looking at the edge of the yard instead of next to the garage, he said, "Well, because there's a streetlamp here, and it's dark by the garage."

We got a nice laugh out of his joke, but then he told us that sometimes we have to search the darkest parts of ourselves to find the keys to our lives. If we only look where we're comfortable looking, we'll miss the most important lessons and never discover our true potential.

My meditation on the previous life where I was hung from my treehouse came down to realizing that I had done this thing, made up this dream, and it is this dream I would undo through forgiveness — not by making the events real, but by undoing that which never took place. Everything in that dream was forgiven by that single lesson once it was truly learned.

I had to learn that both of us — the hangman and the hung — were either guilty or innocent. The one impossible thing was for us to be different from one another. Guilt and innocence cannot both be true. If guilt is true, then God must be fake. If innocence is true, then the guilt must be fake. The mind of God cannot be split.

Epinoia said, "Just what we need: another preacher of hate. 'Sarcasm' comes from the Latin 'tearing the flesh.' It fits pretty well here with your next lesson of forgiveness. You'll see. Remember when you were a preacher of hate? You believed you were taking God's word to a fallen people, people of original sin. You had convinced yourself that you were sent to earth to bring the heathens to justice and make them repent — especially the so-called 'red-skins.' You opened your sermons with characteristic trenchancy, bringing fear to anyone who would listen. Do you recall?"

I'm not sure if that was my next incarnation on this planet, or just the one I remembered next, but it took place in the American Southwest. I was a preacher, although I don't remember of which denomination. I had a small parish in a dusty town built of wood and adobe. The sermons I gave at first were about repentance and taught of an angry god, filled with hate and vengeance. It was the message that I wanted to disseminate at the time. It was also the message my parishioners wanted to hear. I would slam my fist down and scream at the sinners in my view, telling them how much their actions were an abomination to God, and that he cried tears of blood just looking at their wretched souls.

Epinoia continued, "Here, God is angry, yet loving. God is of two minds. God has made you in His image, yet with original sin on your hearts and minds. You tried to bring this same message to the so called 'red-skinned' tribes in the area. You felt it was your duty to bring them to the one true God. Do you recall what happened?"

Yes. A short while after I had settled with my congregation, I met a man who would become my spiritual counselor and God's own agent of mercy and understanding, an old soul who had lived on earth many lifetimes: Whispering Winds. When I say that he was an old soul, I realize that we are all the same age in God's mind, but I use those words to project that he seemed more awake than I was, or than anyone I had seen in that space and time. He called me by the name *One Who Goes with Beauty*, and I spent many nights with him in his village, learning the ways of the spirit and being guided by him. We formed a deep love, and we remain friends to this day. He has transcended this plane, but I can still reach him from time to time when my mind is quiet, and I am at peace. It is impossible to connect with anyone unless you share the same internal vibration, and to reach Whispering Winds requires deep meditation.

His tribe was overrun the same way my tribe had been overrun many continents and life cycles before. Whispering Winds confided that his tribe, many lifetimes and millennia ago, had dominated the continents with a sophisticated and hungry society, and they had oppressed, enslaved, and destroyed other tribes. He told me that he had seen the same angry god I carried in my heart in the men he had lived with many lifetimes before, so he knew where our tribe was headed. He explained that there was no stopping the desires of the hungry ghost, but it is important to pay attention to what we desire instead, adjusting our inner world and letting the outer world take care of itself. He also said that the mind of the *chindi,* or what we would call the devil, is always split, and will always be split. There is no saving the world from the devil; there is only forgiveness and changing our minds about who the devil is. "One Who Goes with Beauty," he said, "look into a still pond with hate in your heart, and the *chindi* will look back at you. Look with only love, and you will see God.

I watched his tribe dwindle and eventually all but disappear. Towards the end, he and I spent long hours in deep meditation, until one eventful night, we were visited by a few members of my old tribe who had helped shepherd many of Whispering Winds' family into a higher plane of existence. I watched with tear-filled eyes as he, too, became translucent, and I felt deep loneliness with his departure.

After he was gone, and his tribe had either left, died, or been assimilated as well as they could into our society, I changed my sermons and started to preach forgiveness and love. It was not well received, and my parishioners became unsettled. Eventually, I was excommunicated. I attempted to make a trek east but froze to death that winter in the Midwest. I can remember feeling very alone and cold, and then suddenly my spirit lifted out of my body, and I floated gently for a while, then skimmed and darted around the earth, until I found my next incarnation in Russia. I didn't realize at the time that I was not yet ready for another pass, and that life ended very early. I spent a lot of time in an orphanage and was finally shot in the back for a loaf of bread and a few coins. Another boy in the orphanage mistakenly thought his salvation depended on a moldy crust of bread I had saved and what amounted to a few pennies. I heard the bang and felt the bullet bite into my skin. I remember the light dimming, and I felt his hands prying my own little hand open, and I felt my pocket being molested. Then I felt nothing for a while.

Epinoia said, "Sometimes life is short, and it is a blessing. That life was a good example. Scarcity is a trick the ego uses to keep egos on edge and in fear. And as a little kid, surrounded by poverty and fear, being shot was not as sad as you might think. Every moment of every day was lived with the sharpness of fear at the surface, raw and piercing. It felt like a giant screaming in your head for you to run, but not telling you where, and then laughing when you froze in panic. Like a bug, thwarted, over in an instant."

I remember the bullet entering my lower back and exiting through my stomach, allowing the tension to escape. The pain I felt was intense, but it faded quickly. What I was left with was a warm blankness. Sometimes life outside a body is without consciousness. It's a momentary gap that doesn't take any shape, color, or size and is gone before it begins. It's what happens to atheists when they die: a wonderful feeling of nothing — but only for a moment. Or when a person commits suicide, the blankness is only momentary, and then the fear of the ego resumes, and it's off again to another life in another body.

Epinoia said, "Scarcity and death are the only two things the ego can be counted on to provide — neither of which is something we want in reality. Our desires are what keeps us coming back again and again. Each visit we make to a body, if it is given to the Holy Spirit, is an opportunity to grow and eventually let the ego slip off, like a snake shedding its skin. And then we are finally free ... unless we chose to believe in death.

"Being a preacher of the god of death will not get you into Heaven. Heaven is now; there is no other time. In fact, there is no time at all. Heaven is here; there is no other place. In fact, again, there is no place at all. God is. If you understand that, then you don't need to say or think anything more.

"You see, my beloved child, God judges with the Holy Spirit the cause of the insanity of this world. But the ego, and what you were running from in loneness when Whispering Winds let go of his ego and slipped into Heaven, is judging the effect. As a preacher, you were telling tales of symptoms that cannot be cured. The secret of salvation is that you are doing all of this to yourself. Rest with that thought for a time and go deeply into your mind. We still have mirrors to visit, but these are reflections of running scared, and the one cure to running in fear is to stop, pause, turn the judgments over to the Holy Spirit, and have the cause healed.

"When you are ready, we'll look at life during death. Or it is death during life? Both? Neither? We shall see."

Chapter 7.

Fall in New York (by Way of Russia)

Epinoia woke me from my meditation with these questions: "What's the worst thing you can think of that can happen to a person in a body? Is it being nailed to a cross? Raped? Murdered? Broken? Having a loved one die? Is it whatever happens to us that we dislike? Being in war? Prison? Is it being a slave to a cruel master who tortures you for your entire life just for fun? Or maybe being homeless? Is it having an experience that others deny?

"Is belief in an untrustworthy god of hatred and resentment to cover for our lack of knowledge that an open mind can offer even worse? There are no levels in hell. So many of your lifetimes were spent wondering how God could allow so much pain and misery to be experienced. Right now, you're thinking of the mirror of complete fear and darkness."

This was a mirror I didn't want to look at, didn't think I was ready for. But Epinoia told me that if I weren't ready, I would not be able to recall those moments. What came to me was that for a time, I had wondered how people could look at life in a body and see anything but pain and misery. The pact we must make to be here is to buy into the ego and accept that death is real, and that there are other people, separate from us, most of whom are only living for material gain or what they can leverage from other people. From the time we are babies, we are little more than one big want. We cry, fuss, and generally try to control our environments until we grow a little and decide we will dominate our environment altogether, or submit to our weakness and quiver in consternation. In this reflection, I was convinced that people are not happy at all, but instead they pretend to be happy, or become convinced that tomorrow will be different. It's like living in a little terrarium, and every day, dinner is dropped in, and you think, *Well, tomorrow I'm sure they will drop in something terrific, much better than today*. But the next day, and the day after that, and on and on, it's the same: "Tomorrow will be better." But it never is. It's always just another shit sandwich.

In that dream, I imagined I lived in New York. I'm not positive, but I think it was in the late 1920s. I was a woman, living scandalously alone and working in an office. To say that I was plain would be kind. Thin, frail, always cold, I wore heavy woolen clothing and small hats with little drab feathers attached even in the warmest days of summer. I walked with my head down and shoulders drooped so that I might disappear altogether. Everything frightened me.

I attended church a few times per week and listened intently to the god of death and hatred. Fear filled my life, but the fear of death was even worse. I had nightmares about being helpless, tortured, and raped, banished to hell for the slightest thought of evil. God is merciful; God is vengeful; God is forgiving; God is angry, and on and on, back and forth. I never once thought to open my mind past an eight-year-old's catechism. My spiritual reflection was that of a frightened child, incapable of thinking for herself.

Everything about that time was dreadful, but beyond the day-to-day drudgery, there came a man with particular malice. He was like a dark, shadowy beast following me to and from work. When I would turn to look at him from the corner of my eye, he would turn away and act as though he were not following me. I would peek out my window in the middle of the night, and there he would be, in a doorway across the street.

This went on for months. I was terrified. I stopped eating and sleeping, and because I had no friends, I was utterly lost in my nightmare. At the time, I felt so uneasy that I started to lose any control of my mind at all. I would slip into cold shivers even in the middle of summer, so I always wore a heavy overcoat. And then without warning, he was gone.

For a while, I started to think that maybe I had made the whole thing up. For a few weeks, I felt as though a fever had lifted. Skeptical of my own thoughts, I would go back and forth: was he real, or had I been making it all up?

It might have been September — or maybe October, I'm sketchy on the details — but I remember it was raining. It had been raining for what felt like weeks. It was a slow, gentle, yet cold rain that seemed to scrub the soul right out of you. I was walking to my apartment when a huge arm covered in a dirty rain slicker reached around and lifted me off my feet, a menacing hug with whisky-and-cigar-smoke breath. I wanted to kick, but my feet were gripped in fear-induced paralysis. I wanted to scream but could not find my voice. My body was frail and light, and I was lifted off the ground like a child.

He carried me up a short flight of stairs, then pushed me against the wall next to my apartment door and held me there with one hand, while digging in my coat pocket for my keys with the other. As I recall it now, my feet were only about an inch off the floor, but they may as well have been a mile in the air for what good they were to me. Then he dragged me inside, pulled out his handkerchief, stuffed it in my mouth, and tied it in place with my scarf.

For the next three or four days, he kept me tied and naked. He would drink and smoke, and then he would fuck me like some crazed beast. I'm not sure how I lived as long as I did. I was dirty, lying in my own pee, with dried semen caked over my lower torso, my breath was shallow, and my wrists and ankles were covered with dried blood. I could feel an ache, like a toothache, but it was throughout my entire body. I wasn't sleeping, but I wasn't completely awake, either. I guess I was drifting in and out. He would rape me, and I would be pulled back into my little body. Then he would leave me, and I would slip away.

Then one day, he stabbed me to death. I remember the knife piercing my skin and the heaviness leaving my body. The sharp pain of the knife only lasted a few seconds, and then nothing. At that moment, I was resolved that God didn't exist at all. My thought was that we are just animals, with the strong preying on the weak. Beasts consume what they want without even a shred of thought for anyone around them.

Maybe there is something to the notion that we use our minds to manifest our deepest desires along with our deepest fears. In that incarnation, it would seem so, although I was gripped with so much fear for so long that I don't recall having any dreams I latched onto that I thought could really come true for me. From a young age, I was launched into a world that seemed completely vicious and cold. So, perhaps it's no wonder it didn't end well. My worries of being raped and murdered were a constant fear for me, and they did eventually come true.

My spirit rose up with the diminishing heat from my emaciated little body and hovered over the corpse for a short while, then drifted off. I was there long enough to watch my murderer masturbate over my now dead body, and I felt a lingering antipathy at the sight. This general feeling of anguish and hatred followed me into the void, and I clung to it like a life raft in the darkness.

Epinoia told me that egos can come into the afterlife without a body. Belief is a thought. Thoughts are things. The difference between belief and knowledge is that belief is a myth; it's a lie. Knowledge is of God. It is the Truth, and the Truth is of God, never changing. In less than a week, I had decided that God didn't exist. How could God allow such horror? The loneliness and dread clung to me, and I placed that at the feet of the god of hate.

Epinoia's voice came to me in that moment, and I was aware that God had never left me. She said, "The god of hate is an atheist. The God of Love is the only thing that is real. Even God is an atheist from the point of view of the ego. If what happened in that life is real, then God must be fake. They cannot both be real. We often ask how God can allow for the terrible things that happen to otherwise good people. How can God allow these awful things to take place without intervening?

"But none of this belongs to God. It's not God who imagines all this hatred and fear. You did that; this was you. You were the rapist and the raped. You were both. Not one or the other, but both. This can be very difficult to realize. We look at ourselves as victims. But the rapist in your dream looked at himself as a victim, too. He had been molested as a child, abused repeatedly, tortured by his parents, society, and everyone around him. He took that shame and pushed it out; he lashed out at this small, cold, lonely woman. When he was finally arrested, several victims later, he cried out, 'But look what they did to me! It's not my fault!'"

As the fear of the moment left, a thought came to mind: *Your own salvation is what you have kept from yourself. It has always been a decision that you can make for yourself.* All the experiences from this so-called life and every other are all the same. They may seem different in their individual moments, but there is only one answer: forgive them, for they know not what they do. Many false dreams, but only one solution: forgive them for that which they never did in reality.

Epinoia said, "Do you remember when we first met? It was between these two lives. Your mind quieted just for a moment, and you were able to listen to me. This was just before your last life — the life with the bus. Do you recall?"

Between this dream and the following dream, I followed the pull of my spirit towards an unborn body. The feeling started as a small tug, easily disregarded. In the void, without a body, the previous death had not been long past, and with that death, I had decided there was no God. But the decisions we make in a body seem more definitive than when we're pure spirit. The mix of spirit and physical body makes us seem more real, and yet we're not as real. There is nothing more real than spirit, and nothing more solid than eternity in God. But earthly desires can have a magic of their own, and it can be very difficult to remember who we really are, especially when we're not in a body. The urge for my spirit to latch onto the base of a spine and draw breath into newly born lungs was very compelling. I felt that I needed to put a form to my anger and hatred.

Chapter 8.

On to the Next Life? (Maybe I Should Have Waited)

For a moment, the anger drained down in me, and out of the void came a voice, coalescing into a single being who was trying desperately to slow down my skimming from life to death and back again. Out of the mists of my running, angry dream, gently, quietly, a small voice of love and encouragement came to me with a message that nearly stopped this incarnation, and which followed me into my new body, seating itself as a pure white aura around me.

You know you don't have to do this. You don't have to take on another body, only to be disappointed again. Nobody is chasing you. You have lived out many thousands of lives, running from one body to the next, hiding out for a short time, only to come back here again and again. God isn't angry with you. The truth is that God has only love for you and holds the memory of you as it was first thought. All you need is to awaken to your true self, and this insane dream of yours will end, and you will be with God, eternally loved. It's a simple decision.

"You're a woman?"

Is that what you think? I had wondered. My presence will give you comfort, and I cannot cause you any more fear than you already have; it's just not in our nature to do so. So, female must be what makes you most comfortable. But no, gender is meaningless to us. It only means something to your dreaming mind.

Everything you need to learn about your true self can be learned here, with us. Take a pause, and you may stay as long as you like. There is no rush to move on. Time for you is no longer linear, as it is in physical form. Everything you believe about time has no meaning here. Time isn't controlling you here. This newborn body will wait. Or you may take another body. The decision is yours. The pain and suffering of this life will not include your own guilt. You will not imagine that you requested any of this for yourself. This is how illusions are born. You are making all this up, but you will not see yourself as making this up, and the experience will not depend on your awareness of your role in the process.

"But I made a pact to go back. I feel the urge to return, to get this right. This is the life where I will succeed. Now is the time."

That's your ego calling you. Your ego tells you that you need to be a body. It tells you that you're not complete — and if you believe it, you will center your mind on a new body and tumble back into the fantasy of human flesh. You've been so many different beings: finned creatures, winged creatures, furry creatures, and most recently, a woman on Earth. But there is nothing for you to get right that cannot be completed here, with us, in a gentle and loving way. The choice is yours, between a nightmare of death and suffering, and a happy awakening of joy and life.

"That last life was a mistake. I should have been a man, so I could have protected myself. I just need to be stronger."

Oh, beloved, if you could just for one Holy Instant stop running, you would understand that salvation is not something you can fight for, or run to, or find on a quest. Salvation is already yours, just for being an idea in God's mind. There is nothing to learn, no one to fight for or against, no one who needs protection. Attack doesn't exist in reality, and no harm can come to who you really are.

"The pull, the draw is strong. I must go soon.

"... Are you still there? I'm afraid."

I know you're afraid, my beloved. But we never leave. It's you who thinks we leave. But we're always together. We're always with you. When you go, remember, you are not a body; you are as God created you: a spirit on a human journey. You will be in the world, but never of it. And when you allow your mind to rest, you can always hear us; you can hear the voice of God. When you're calm, the voice will come to you. Let God lead you, and you cannot fail. Align your will with God, and the way will be clear. Know that we, that God, loves you. We are all One with you. When you are calm, you will hear us...

The voice faded as my spirit drifted back towards an earthly body. It would take me more than half my life to remember these loving words, and another decade after that to hear the voice again. It would seem that when we enter a body, we forget nearly everything.

I asked Epinoia if that had been her, and she told me it was. Her voice did seem familiar. I told her for the first time that I loved her.

Chapter 9.

Mommy's Little Angel

When we attach to a body, the spirit is not in the body, but the body is in the mind of the spirit. We are not born, and we do not die. But it sure seems that way, doesn't it? No matter how often I tried to remember that when I was in a body, the idea that the body isn't real doesn't make any sense with a shallow look.

Some of my earliest thoughts in this life cycle were of addiction. I spent my time in my mother's womb going from one drunken binge and nicotine panic to another. I was not oblivious to the fights between my mother and father, and I can remember feeling as though I had made a terrible mistake in coming here. Fear was what I felt — that, and hungover most of the time, and the nicotine fits would have me spinning. The light of my soul hovered around the frail little body, hesitating, and at the last moment, it seemingly slipped into the lower spine, creating the kundalini, popping out the chakras and filling the body with life.

Some think the body is the whole thing — that your brain is the house that holds your essence. Scientists poke and prod brain tissue like monkeys with a stick. "Oh, look, I poke over here, and that little thing moves! The brain must be who we are." They never stop to think that perhaps the brain is in your mind — that maybe they have the whole thing backwards.

Epinoia said, "The body is a tool, a communication device, and a way for us to find forgiveness and realize our true nature. We are not bodies. We are free of the constraints that seem to hold us in a limited, meaty carcass dependent on clothing, food, and shelter to survive. Except we aren't bodies just clunking around. Just because we believe we are the product of birth in a body, and that we had nothing to do with that birth — that it was not our decision at all — doesn't make it true. Furthermore, many believe that God created this system, perhaps as a punishment, perhaps as his way of sorting out his good works from his bad works. Some try to explain our world by saying, 'God works in mysterious ways' and creates unlike Itself, that God can create a place that is unequal and savage, and that it is possible for God to create the opposite of love, or that our own free will is stronger than God's Will for us.

"This is all insanity, of course. We project all of this with our thoughts. We create a world that lacks any kind of forgiveness, and fill it with darkness and hate and fear for an insignificant god of ego — a psychopathic god who would create a person in a body that will eventually die, with a propensity for pain and suffering, with desires in themselves that draw them towards all manner of insult and injury, on a spinning little rock of a planet as far from the center of the universe as it can be, which wobbles on its axis, overheats, overcools, and creates events that tear though it, destroying everything in their path. And at the same time, this same bipolar god insists we either love him, or he'll show us what real hell is. And we let the fear well up in our hearts without stopping for just one second and asking the Holy Spirit for guidance."

That was meant for me in this life. It's what I thought for many, many lifetimes. I believed that God was chasing me — that God was really pissed, that I had committed some terrible sin, and that I needed to be punished. The guilt was so overwhelming that I spent many thousands of lifetimes going from one terrible nightmare to another, from victim to perpetrator and back again.

In this incarnation, it was a hot summer day when my mother ventured off to go shopping. She was pregnant but determined to walk to a department store. As she made the journey, her water broke, and a few hours later, I slipped out of her. And while I was not ready for this life, my soul seemed to slip into a tiny body, and once that connection was made, I would become an angelic little boy with lily-white skin and tiny grey-green jewels for eyes.

Had I been able to talk when I was born, my first words would have been, "I need a smoke and a shot of gin." But I wasn't able to talk, and the feeling was a crawling, itchy, skin-piercing sharpness, a desire at my very core that would be transformed into a wild panic and put a target on my tiny little back that would attract all kinds of misguided parasites in human form. I would turn to nearly anything to fill this desire to self-medicate, which would take me down some very dark paths and lead to all manner of indulgences over the years.

Everything was blurry at first, and then the great forgetting took place. Smells and sounds were muffled, and there was a deep sense of aloneness. The illusion of separation lay on me like midsummer humidity sticks to heavyset people. The constant want lodged in the midst of my tiny body, and then the ego sprang to life, promising to save me. It cried out, screaming its demands and taking over the body to direct it, help it survive, and convince me that it was real.

There were two nurses who looked like tall, white ghosts, with pale skin that was nearly translucent. Imagine someone who has never been in the sunlight, and you'll understand the near greyness of their complexion. I don't remember any smiles, although I suppose at some point there were some. What I remember instead was the coldness of being carried off, scrubbed, and wrapped. And from then until I was about four years old, I had the sense of being outside my body. It was as though I were slightly behind and above, but not inside looking out. And while I now know most of what happened in those early years that caused my aura to slip away like that, and even though the kundalini was secured, committing me to this illusion, the pain and chaos were too great for my spirit to reside here comfortably. I remember thinking before I was born, and then even more as a little boy, that I should not have come when I did — and while I know why I did, and it makes sense now in the house of mirrors, I can also say that it was painful beyond my own imagining.

While I was mommy's sweet little angel, if you are sensitive to child abuse, you may want to skip this part. I'm honest about the events that took place. They may be disturbing, but when we dislodge our ego mind, it can often happen with great pain and suffering. That can happen especially to the most innocent of us.

Chapter 10.

What Could be Worse?

The house was quiet in the early evening. Winter, spring, summer, and fall all blended together like one big fuzzy blanket of time. The house creaked and groaned, and my brother and I were alone with a very disturbed foster child named Linda. She hated my brother because he could talk. She loved me because I couldn't. I was also one of those babies that people stop to look at and want to hold. I was tiny, and I didn't cry or fuss much. I looked like a little blond angel. I could hold my head up, but I didn't move much. My mother said I looked like a little doll, and she would take me on walks around town to show me off to people, and those people, especially women and girls, would beg to hold me.

The sun had settled behind the trees outside my room, and I was lying in my crib, waiting for Linda to come up the stairs. I could hear my mother and father giving her instructions before they went out for the night, leaving my brother and me alone with Linda for the evening. My parents would be out until midnight, at least. My spirit was hovering over my bed, and my tiny body was anxious for Linda to come up the stairs. Then I felt the door close, and the atmosphere changed in my room, and the curtains gently heaved in and out as though the house were drawing a breath.

When Linda ran up the stairs, I watched as my body twitched. She walked across the room, slowing down as she came closer. My arms extended, and my body started to kick and rock. She cooed and reached over the gates of my crib. My body knew what was coming, and my spirit watched patiently, knowing what was about to happen as well. My spirit wanted to whisk my body up and hide it from her. But my little body wanted what she was about to do to me.

Linda danced my body around the room, twirling and rocking. Then she felt my diaper, which would have still been dry from a recent changing by my mother. My spirit witnessed the darkness coming over Linda, her eyes dilated, and her anticipation flowered like a black rose. She was maybe twelve or thirteen, so she didn't understand what she was doing to me, and she couldn't control the forces driving her, etched there by someone when she had been not much older than I was then. An evil gift passed down from one ego to the next, a sloppy, dirty present wrapped in hatred and confusion, and given without mindfulness from one itchy, addicted, struggling ego to another.

She was completely lost in her excitement, and my tiny body was completely at her disposal. She placed me on the bassinette and took off my diaper. My spirit watched as my body wiggled and then went calm the moment she touched me. She rubbed me and excited my body hundreds of times over the next year — and I became addicted to the feelings she unleashed inside me. The fight for my atonement started when I was no more than two.

The abuse slowed down my attachment to this body and led the way to a very profound understanding of guilt, shame, and recovery. For that, I am grateful. That sounds funny now, even to me, but without that insanity, I would never have been able to understand the ego as well as I do now. The human desires were amplified to the point that I could not ignore them. Many lifetimes are spent thinking things are going to get better, or maybe for some, even become great. The thought can be of success in moving through this world. But that's just an egotistical illusion. Nothing in this world can ever become great, because none of it is real.

Chapter 11.

Excommunicated at Such an Early Age

Flash forward several years, still in this same nightmare. Being pushed out of the Catholic nest at a delicate age was the worst thing that could have happened to me — even worse than being sexually abused. Okay, that's a lie, really. But if I had to pick one, the spiritual torture took longer to forgive. It's a lie, because all suffering is the same. Whether a needle poke in the toe, the sexual abuse of an infant, or the spiritual abuse of a young boy, it's all the same.

To start with, I don't remember being in catechism before my first Communion. What I remember was being hit in the head with a wet sponge, lobbed from the front of the classroom at a Catholic school, for not paying attention well enough. And there is the faintest of dark spots on my memory of a hateful message being tossed at my consciousness, but nothing really stuck there. It's as though the wet sponge and the Catholic faith bounced off and evaporated together.

Thinking about it now, I'm happy that I was in a haze back then from being molested and picked on unmercifully, or I might have taken the few lessons offered by the black-and-white penguins at the front of the room more seriously. It was a message of fear and hate that has been handed down and revised for many thousands of years. Well before their Mr. Jesus came along to try to straighten them out, and based on what little I did hear, it was obvious that they themselves had not learned anything from their savior at all.

If you understood just how deep your hate is that is buried in your ego — how deep my hatred was as well — you would completely freak out. You'd understand why you run, skipping from one body to the next, from one miserable mess to another, denying it ever happened. It's like a continuous drama played out through eternity, poorly acted and presented with stale refreshments. But once you remember God's Love, even for the tiniest moment, you suddenly realize everything we make is pain. Eating, dressing, sex, jokes, parties... Even getting your own way is painful. Our egos try to convince us that we love the nightmare, but that's a lie we tell ourselves to keep us from reality. The truth is that we are all-powerful and much stronger than the insanity we shroud around our strength to act all innocent of our role in this or any other life. We make up the lives we live, projecting them out of our borrowed minds. We are faux gods, yet real Gods in training.

The Catholic myth that bounced off me in catechism would finally be driven into me with a long, bony finger and all the hatred a Midwestern priest could muster in the back of a church on a Sunday morning. It was a sunny day, and I was rousted out of bed and dressed in clothing that rubbed and scratched and told that I couldn't eat until after church. I felt anxious, but I didn't know what I was afraid of. You know the feeling you get when you can't find your purse or wallet? It was a little like that, only I wasn't sure what I was missing.

My dad's Dodge Monaco station wagon sat burbling in the driveway, with my brothers and sister already dressed and waiting as I scurried up from my basement bedroom, feeling hungry and itchy in dress pants that never fit at the waist or inseam because they were hand-me-downs from an older brother who was both shorter and heavier than me. My dad's face was red with anger as he threatened me with a smack on the ass if I didn't 'get the fuck in the car' that moment. As soon as I shut the door, my dad's foot planted itself on the accelerator, spitting gravel from our driveway and tossing me off the seat and onto the floor. My father had turned his body and wrapped his arm around the passenger seat so he could look out the back window as he sped down our driveway in reverse, and he couldn't resist stabbing the back of my shaved head with the tips of his fingers while I recovered from my tumble. The sudden sharp pain caused my arms to fly up around my head for protection, and that, coupled with his sudden braking, caused my head to bobble back and forth, hammering the seat and seat back, making me dizzy. "Get the hell off the floor! What the fuck is your problem?" he shouted.

You know how some days just start poorly and then fall into the abyss? I listened to a recording of Earl Nightingale years later, and in it he suggested that a person should change their thinking to recover the rest of the day. When things go wrong right away, like if you stub your toe, you have a decision to make about the rest of your day, and you can either let it slide further down the drain by doing nothing but bitching about your toe, or you can choose to change the direction of the day with your mind by refocusing your thoughts.

But it wasn't my toe that was the problem, and I didn't have access to what my father would have called 'the wishful thinking of a snake oil salesman,' so you need to multiply a toe-stubbing by hacking off the leg at the knee with a rusty hatchet in order to only begin to understand my first Communion. The short ride to the church was not long enough to allow the head-banging to fade before we were being herded into the hard oak pews soaked with incense. The smell of a church is probably the most hateful thing there is in my memory of that lifetime, and it still might overwhelm me the moment I walk through the doors of an old house of worship. The smoky, gagging stench of stale incense, sweet perfume, flatulence, and the lingering psychopathic god of hate reaches into my nostrils and pulls the trigger of an ancient fear that wells up in me, taking me back to the tiny mad thought that we could ever be separate from our Beloved.

After a blurred sermon, all the new Catholics were lined up in the aisle and led back into the apse of the church. The kid behind me asked if I had a good sin to share. I panicked, thinking that I didn't know I was supposed to bring something, and while I didn't know what a sin was, I knew for certain I didn't have one and didn't know where to get one on such short notice. I searched my little disturbed brain for anything that I might offer as a sin but drew a blank.

The walk into the back of the church was both short and eternal. Like watching roller coaster carts tumble off the edge of the first dive before my eyes, I watched a string of well-dressed children walk into darkness, the fading light glowing on their obligatory whiteness. The apse was dark except for a few glowing stained glass windows depicting Jesus nailed up on a wooden cross and tortured, and a few tiny red candles that looked like flickering little hard candies lined up on a rack of wooden shelves. We all stood in a neat little line and waited. Then a black-and-white penguin woman marched past the front of the line, tugging and folding our hands into a submissive prayer position and telling us not to slump, but to keep our heads down, hands clenched together like little slaves ready to meet the god of hate in the flesh. And in fact, I expected God to come out of the sacristy at any moment.

I stood there with the other neophytes, searching for a sin and beating myself up for not asking anyone if I had to have something to share or pass on or give as a gift, or at least asking if anyone had an extra sin I could use. It would be a good six months after my first Communion that I would go to the library and search for anything I could find about sins and what they meant, and why I was supposed to bring one to church with me. I read everything I could get my hands on about sin, both for and against. Honestly, I was way more open to the arguments against than those for. Most of what I read about sin was depressing for a little kid who had been banished from the church — at least, as much as I understood, since I struggled with reading until well into college.

When the priest came out of the sacristy, all our little heads shot up like startled prairie dogs, then dropped down again in remembrance of the beatings and scolding from the penguins standing behind us. I was determined to figure out what a sin was, so I was hypervigilant, looking for any clue I could find. I was glad to be in the middle of the line rather than on the end nearest the sacristy door. As the priest moved closer to me, a new panic washed over the old panic, because I couldn't speak Greek or Latin, the two languages the priest was using, and the kids were so afraid that they were speaking just above a whisper, so I couldn't hear what they were saying.

Had the other kids been speaking louder, I would have realized that they were each sharing their own special sins that they all had been prompted to tell the priest, probably by their parents, to prove they understood their imperfection. But since they were all speaking so quietly, I only heard the kid next to me say, "Uh, I, ah, took a nickel off my dad's dresser, and um, uh … I took my brother's bike without, um, telling him." And then the priest said something in Greek or Latin again, and my friend opened his mouth like a little baby bird, and the faux god gave him a little white disc on his wet pink tongue and shuffled in front of me. I thought that must be the sin I needed. And so, I gave the very same one, including the ums, errs, and pauses that the kid next to me had uttered. I figured the sin must be said in a certain way, or it wouldn't have any magical powers to make the priest release his little white disc and move on to the next kid.

The apse of the church seemed like a castle to me. The ceilings were so high that I would sometimes sit in the pews and imagine hanging from the wooden beams, pretending I was a monkey, swinging back and forth and then launching my agile little body from the rafters to the huge hanging brass light fixtures, lulling myself into a bored dream state someplace between sleep and awake that would pry open the wall between conscious and subconscious, letting my imagination run as far from church and its darkness as dreams could take me. Sometimes the monkey would make each jump like an Olympic gymnast. Other times, the monkey would just miss the hanging lamp, losing his grip, tumbling down and bouncing off a bouffant, hat, or bonnet, landing gracefully on his feet and taking a bow. Then he would scurry up the huge wooden columns and launch himself up onto the sad and lonely sculptures of ancient white people locked in sour frowns, climbing gracefully back up into his rafters and giant lights. You can probably see why I didn't have a sin to tell. Almost all my class and church attendance was spent in much the same way. My mind would slip away from the pain and boredom of a Victorian-style lecture and race off to faraway places, until puberty set in, and then my mind would run up some girl's skirt instead.

But during the moment of silence between my stolen and real sins, the moment of pause that followed the final echo of my voice — a child's voice that sprung up right behind the kid next to me and launched the most terrifying reaction I have ever heard before or since — a short and ever-so-innocent feeling of accomplishment swept over me, clearing out the fear of not knowing what a sin was, to thinking I knew what a sin was, to being sure I didn't know anything about sin. I slowly looked up at the priest, keeping my head down and my hands clasped in front of me in innocent submission.

What I saw was at once familiar and as scary as anything that could crawl out through the gates of a dark nightmare: a pasty-white face without expression suddenly realizing what I had said and slowly transforming into a cracked porcelain statue that had jumped down off the walls of the church and discovered the most loathsome child in existence. He stooped down to my level and opened his mouth in slow motion, taking in a deep breath of stale, incense-drenched air, and for a moment, I thought I recognized him. He looked like Dr. Seuss's Grinch, only completely absent of any coloration other than the thin, weak blue lines of veins that started to pulsate and expand with his rage — a white Grinch sent to drag little boys who lie during their initiation into the one true church down into hell, where they would suffer for all eternity.

Once the air was driven down into his skinny chest, it came back out as a string of warnings, condemnations, and prophecies about my future, and that of my entire family. At the same time, he jerked his bony, chalky fingers into my chest and started poking and punching me backwards, his mouth moving rapidly, spit spraying over me. He told me that I was going straight to hell and taking my entire family with me. There was no hope for me, and I was such a horrible creature that even Satan would kick me to the curb. If there was a hell that Satan couldn't go to, that's where I deserved to be, for the entirety of all time and beyond. If Satan has a list of bad boys and girls, my name was now at the very top, underlined in blood-red ink, and neither the angels nor the god of hate could erase it.

I walked backwards, and he yelled and told me to stand still, while at the same time pushing me backwards until I was pressed up against a wall. My arms fell to my sides, and I turned my head to keep his stale breath and moist spittle from landing directly on my face. I could not think. My little body started to shake, and I lost control of my bladder for a moment, then caught it again. It was like the air was suddenly sucked out of my lungs and into the pasty little godhead raging in front of me.

Have you ever had a panic attack? I ask you that because then you can just begin to know what I felt in that moment. I couldn't catch my breath. My heart was beating like a hammer in my chest. Adrenaline was pulsating through me, making me want to run as fast as I could to anywhere but where I was. If I could have willed myself to explode in that moment, I would have done it, with the hopes of killing him and myself at the same time, dragging us both into the depths of hell. If he had sexually molested me — as he was later accused of doing — I would have recovered more quickly. In fact, his sexual advances would have blended into the earlier molestations, and I might have forgotten the whole thing. Instead, I spent countless nights fearing the darkness, convinced that the devil would come for me at any moment. Any slight adjustment in light or an unexpected movement from anyone I was near would send an electric pulse through my body, and a flash would spring into my head of bleached bone arms splitting the earth, grabbing me by the legs, and pulling me down. I was unable to watch any horror movies or TV shows, or even cartoons like *Scooby-Doo*. They were just too real for me. And in my mind, the monsters were never as frightening as the caricatures behind the creatures, which all resembled the monsignor who had excommunicated me.

It has since occurred to me that if I'd actually had a good sin to tell — one that the priest approved of, one that he would have recognized as my own original experience rather than the one I snatched out of the mouth of my classmate — my search for the truth probably would have ended there, as with so many young people. The priest would have wrapped his truth in incense-soaked, wine-stained, ancient horror stories and passed them on to me, embedding them in my fragile little brain to harden and become second nature. I would have stopped thinking and searching for the truth and would have swallowed the lies of the ego, like so many religious people today who club anyone near them with fear and hatred when asked the simplest of questions regarding the insanity of their faith.

It would never have occurred to me that the Truth — God's Truth — was available to me if only I could empty my mind and let reality seep in. The world we see isn't real. The stories we've been told about God are not true, either. And what we call sin isn't real; it's a man-made threat that expresses the fear and loathing we feel for ourselves. Sin is a shroud we place over our True nature, the nature that God gave us, the power God instilled in us that we are terrified of. The meaning of the word *sin* should be changed to 'lack of love,' because the god of hate preaches the lack of love. The god of hate is a story of a psychotic mind in conflict over everything it has created.

If I were standing with the priest right now, today, looking him in the eye, confessing my sins, he would probably like what I would say even less now than he did then. I imagine him grabbing his heart, his twisted, starched face turning from anger to horror as the words tumble out of my mouth. "Bless me, father, for I have made a mistake about sin. Sin is insanity, the means the ego uses to drive perfect minds mad. It's how we let illusions take the place of Truth: echoes of a twisted mind filled with guilt and shame. Sins are arrogance used as proof that God doesn't exist. Sin keeps us from realizing our true identity. Sins keep us from accepting the gifts God has given us and trick us into believing our will is stronger than God's. As a part of God's Mind, if I have sinned, father, then God must also hold sin in Its Mind, but because God is sinless, then so must I be sinless."

Epinoia spoke: "Jesus didn't come here to die for our sins, and God didn't send Him here to die for any of us. Jesus came to show us that death doesn't exist. To be in awe of Jesus is to allow the ego to keep us from getting near to Him. He is our brother, and what He achieved is what He is trying to help us achieve.

"Bless you, father, for thinking that anyone could sin, for teaching that anyone could be anything other than what

God created. I forgive you for falling into the trap of the ideas of the ego."

I have mixed feelings about what the priest did, what he said, and what he started that day. On the one hand, I felt so much fear that it's still difficult to express. Yet I never would have found God without being kicked out of the church at an early age. As I forgive him, I forgive myself for that which never happened, because it was a powerful illusion, but as ephemeral as anything we call life, and still a starting point for my search for Truth. Seek, and you will find, but you must first be open to the Truth without illusion. Open your mind, father, for you are God in disguise.

But alas, I wasn't an adult. I was a seven-year-old child being spiritually tortured by an insane old preacher in a faith so twisted and out of touch with reality that it would not only allow for that kind of abuse, but instead, it condoned and trained priests to administer it with reverence and passion.

The humiliation of being called out in front of my peers hung on me like cigar smoke on an old sweater. It was moist and thick, as if the priest's words had been made of dirty molasses that clung to me. The other kids kept their distance, and I kept my head down as I walked back to my parents in the back of the church. I could not bring myself to look at them directly. For the first time in my life, I knew a great horror about them — no, had brought a great horror on them, and they were oblivious to it. They were all going to hell, and I had sent them there.

My father, still angry, sat with a frown on his face. My mother, always wearing his anger as carried guilt, sat staring straight ahead. My brothers and sister fidgeted in their seats, wishing time would move more quickly. For them, time had spun to a halt, crawling like a white-haired old lady in the Buick her husband left her, as the hardwood pew pulsated pain into their flesh. But for me, time was whirring too quickly, tumbling forward like an out-of-control wagon flung down a steep hill, taking with it any hope of a childhood.

Truth be told, I didn't really like my family all that much. But now that I had dragged them into Satan's outstretched arms, I suddenly felt responsible for them in a way no seven-year-old should ever experience. I glanced in quick peeks at them out of the corner of my eye, looking to see if they knew. What I saw was unhappiness, and I imagined each was wishing the event were over. But unlike me, it was just boredom that had them wanting an end to the mass. For me, it was fear, and a sense that I needed to find this Satan fellow and try to reason with him. That, or try to explain to him that the priest had gotten it all wrong and it was all just a big mistake, or to beg my family out of the predicament I had brought on them. My little molested brain was already busy recounting everything the bony priest had said to me. An echo of hateful words bounced around in my head, each being searched for anything that might offer a way out. There must have been something in his angry tantrum that would offer a way to forgiveness. God was, after all, merciful. Isn't that what the priest would say from time to time? Just ask for forgiveness, and that's all that matters. Except he only said that occasionally — maybe once in every thousand times that he said we were all sinners and deserved to be punished. And there wasn't anything I could hang onto that he had said that sounded anything at all like merciful.

I moved very quickly beyond looking for an out to looking for a way to either reason with this devil person or maybe find a way to fight back, or at least make a deal of some kind.

The fear made the next several months blurry. My family stopped going to church altogether. I thought it was because I had gotten us thrown out. Regardless, the same dreadful priest who had condemned my entire family to hell because of my stolen sin would spend the next several Saturdays in my parents' living room, drinking my parents' booze and arguing with my father. I would sit at the top of the stairs and listen to their fights and shouts, billows of confused arguments mixed with cigarette smoke rolling over me, burning my eyes, causing me to tear up and making my head spin. Then after they were done arguing, my dad would pluck the priest's bicycle off the gravel, toss it in the back of his Monaco station wagon, and burble him back down our driveway, spitting gravel off towards the church, because the monsignor was too drunk to pedal his three-wheeled bicycle the four or five blocks back to the rectory.

I was convinced all their arguments were about me. How could they not be? I had caused trouble for my family, so grievous that there was no way to correct it. I imagined my father was arguing for his and my salvation to an unmoved audience who was hardened in his judgment against me. And on his return, when I would ask my father what they were arguing about, he would slur a dismissive answer. "You wouldn't understand. Go find some kids to harass and get your royal-natured ass out of my house."

But the real reason for the man's smoky, drunken visits was a mixture of a priest's desire to drink and smoke away a Saturday afternoon, and because that same angry priest had insisted that my father share his tax returns to prove he was tithing the required ten percent. It had been a money call with benefits, and my father, seething with anger at the audacity of this "bony little shit-bag, to think he could just waltz into his house and insist on seeing his sacred tax returns" only ended when my father kicked him out once and for all and pulled our family out of the church altogether. Sadly, he never shared his reasons with anyone, not even my mother, that I can recall. So, of course, I thought it was I who had gotten us pushed out of the supportive nest of the Catholic church.

For a little kid, us leaving the church so abruptly was a traumatic experience. I took the entire mischief on my own shoulders, thinking I was the reason we were no longer members of the Catholic society. At the time, I could not see how perfect or precious that experience was. It forced me to turn inward for answers. It forced me to grow up spiritually. More importantly, the experience led me to forgive God. I know that sounds funny, but it is an essential step in spiritual growth. The god of the ego is cruel beyond anything we can imagine, or at least take responsibility for. When Epinoia asked what is the absolute worst thing that can happen to a human being, for me, it is being indoctrinated into a faith of fear and hatred. The worst thing that can happen to a mind attached to a body is to be led to believe that you are born with original sin. To be taught you are unworthy of the Love of God is a mistake beyond any comparison.

Epinoia said, "A lucid dream that you believed was beyond your control. Setting this up as a child, you could imagine you were a part of someone else's dream and had no control over what was happening to you. You were an innocent child, with no power over your circumstances, and your father and the priest had all the control. It was their doing, not yours. The miracle of forgiveness here is not to awaken you from the dream necessarily, but instead, to show you that you were the dreamer of the dream. You had a choice of dreams while you were still asleep. Did you want to dream of death, and the hateful god of punishment? Or healing and God-Love? All dreams in a body share a memory that features what you wanted shown to you.

"What the priest and your father misunderstood was that they are both the Sons of God, and God is the Father by way of His Sons and Daughters. God cannot be the Father or Mother without the extension of Its Children. What you misunderstood is that none of this happened to you. Any form of attack or judgment by the ego is a meaningless attempt to give effects to the causeless and make it become a cause. Father is Father because of You, in Your True Mind. God is God because of You.

"Sit with this for a bit and remember the *cause* that fear was made to undo. In the stillness, remember what was before your own dream that came to stand between the present and the past to shut down your memory of Who You are in Reality. Also imagine the priest in this dream as a person you hate still, and focus on him as he was to you then. As you do, allow your mind to show you the light in him. Perhaps it's just a glimmer of God's Love. As the spark of light expands around him, for the first time in all sincerity, you can now see him as your savior. Not because of what he did in that lifetime, but because he is your Brother in Love."

Chapter 12.

Are You Afraid of the Dark?

Epinoia said, "What happened after you left the church in your youth in that lifetime? The darkness of myths of magic descended on your home, didn't it? Your mother brought mystical experiences into your house, and with it came a fear of the dark. Are you still afraid of the dark? Do you still cling to the belief in death as a cold, dark place where the undeserving go to suffer? Do you still believe in ghosts? Be thankful you had a mother who did, or you may never have faced your fear of the dark."

It was only a few weeks later that the crystal ball showed up in our house. I remember when I first saw it. It was heavy and milky white, and my mother kept a velvet cloth over it. It sat in the middle of the dining room table, resting on a metal stand over a little old-fashioned embroidered cloth. At first, I didn't know what it was or what it was for, so I thought it was cool, perfectly round and so heavy. My mother would holler at me to keep my hands off it, that my greasy hands would keep it from working. And it wasn't until a few weeks later that I would discover what it was for, and I would take it on as my archenemy.

"What does it do, Mom?"

"Nothing. You wouldn't understand, and it's not for you anyway, so leave it."

I hated those words. Nothing made me feel more frustrated than someone telling me that I wouldn't understand. When someone said that, I felt stupid, like maybe there were things in the world that were truly beyond my comprehension. Of course, if she would have said what it was for, I might have grabbed it off the table and taken it out to the garage and smacked it to pieces with a hammer. Had I known then what it was, I would have used any means possible to make sure it was never unleashed in our house.

One night — it had to be a Friday or Saturday, because my parents had invited people over, and they only did that on weekends — I was shaken from a deep sleep by a terrible nightmare. This wasn't unusual; I would have a nightmare nearly every other day. But what made this one more disturbing is that it seemed so real. You know how most dreams are not vivid at all, and they come across sort of like watching an odd, boring play through a dirty window with muffled sound? And then, every once in a while, you have a dream that seems more real than waking life, as though the colors and images are more intense than anything you've ever seen before? Well, this nightmare was like that. It seemed real, and when I woke up, I could hear what sounded like static electricity being peeled off my body and saw flashes of light around my bed and little creatures scattering off in all directions.

I lay in my bed for a moment, too scared to move. I thought if I just stayed completely quiet, whatever it was that I saw would not find me. But after a time, I decided to get up and look for my parents, or at least my mother. My father would be angry that I was awake, irritated that I was a living, breathing person who might have a problem that would require his attention. As I think about it now, he always seemed angry or put out in some way, like he would have preferred that I didn't exist. It's like he could just look at you and make you feel like you didn't belong anywhere — not just in his presence, but that you didn't belong anywhere at all. *Contempt* is the word that fits here, if contempt were a wet blanket that you could lay over someone and make it stick there, or plastic wrap that sticks with static electricity. It was as if his looking at you could steal your very soul. Or maybe it was a competitive thing, like my brothers and sisters and I were taking his wife for our mother against his will, like he was telling us that he wasn't done with her yet, and we had no claim to her.

Apprehensive, I stepped as quietly as I could, not sure that I wanted to be with my father, and at the same time, wanting some reassurance that everything was going to be okay from my mother. I could hear my mother's voice mumbling and chanting as I got closer to the dining room. I couldn't make out what she was saying, but as I rounded the corner, what I saw was my mother at the head of the dining room table with my father and their friends all around, and the crystal ball in the middle of the table. And standing behind my mother, like he was stuck to the wall, off the ground, just hanging there, was a wispy little man who looked like the ghost of the priest who had condemned me to hell.

The hair on the back of my neck stood on end. It was obvious to me that they couldn't see him, but I could. They were all looking at the ball, which was glowing a little, not by itself, but mostly from all the candlelight in the room. The air left my lungs, and my little body froze in fear. At that moment, I was about as scared as I thought it was possible to be. But a moment later, the ghost of the priest turned his white, skeletal head towards me — and smiled. Well, not really smiled; it was more of a grin. If my fear had already been at level ten, when that little shit-bag looked at me, my panic and horror leapt off the charts.

When you see ghosts in the movies, they don't look like that in real life. I've never seen a ghost done well in film. They don't glow, so much as they pull light from everything around them, making everything outside their ghostly space duller and less clear. It's like they're sucking energy out and away, a little like watching water run over a dam. If you look at the water in its aggregate — not each stream, but the entire massive sheet all at once — and let it mesmerize you, that's more what it looks like, except the ghost is not moving, just still.

"Honey, what are you doing up?" My mother got up from her chair. The little priestly ghost swirled around her movement, back into the center of the room, and was gone.

"Why the fuck are you out of bed?" My father, always angry, never wanting to be interrupted, stood up and came towards me from the other side of the table. "Get back in bed, now! What is your problem?"

Before my father could reach me and swat my backside, my mother had my hand and was leading me back to my bedroom.

Walking down the hall, I asked, "What were you doing in there?"

"Nothing. Nothing you would understand. Now get back into bed and go to sleep."

But I did understand. I understood plenty — perhaps more than she did.

"Who was that little man standing behind you?"

"What little man? You mean the neighbors?"

"No, not them. The one sitting on the wall, over your shoulder."

My mother had lifted me back into bed, and she put her hands at my sides and just stared at me. I could tell that it scared her a little that something she had conjured had floated out behind her and she hadn't seen it.

"There wasn't anything behind me; it was dark in there. Now go to sleep." She kissed my forehead and tuned toward the door.

"I know what I saw. It was that mean man from the church — the one who hates me, the one who hollers at Dad."

She stopped for a moment but didn't turn around. "Nobody hates you. Now go to sleep." And she was gone.

My mother could do that: just tune you out. It was like if she said something didn't happen because she hadn't seen it herself, just her telling you otherwise made what you said not real. Except this time, I knew what I had seen, and I didn't like it one bit. That creepy little priest was haunting us. And I was determined to exorcise that miserable demon if I had to drag him out into the street and pound him with my bare hands.

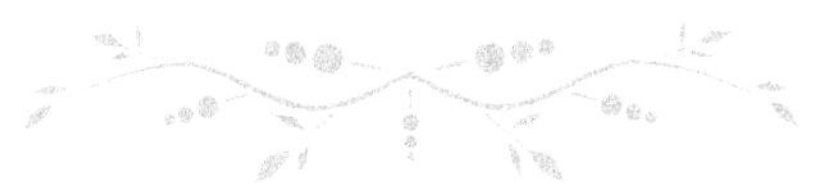

Chasing down the devil at a young age isn't done directly, but rather through self-fulfilling prophecies. That's primarily because a child's brain isn't solidified yet, so it's not logical or direct. At least, mine wasn't. My brain was more elastic and imaginative. But at the base of my mind, even then, I knew that I was connected to God like an ancient mystic, able to travel and create and connect with the Divine Presence that surrounds all of us. My intuition has always been powerful, and my spirit guides and higher teachers have been near me, reminding me that my purpose here is to transcend the long and tragic string of lifetimes I have created, bouncing like a monkey from one shattered imaginary life to the next. My mission was and is to live the last few slow burns of hell and emerge as a transcended being, able to help others find their way to the real world, the permanent embrace of God's Love, and discover their inheritance: the promise God made through the Holy Spirit, and that Jesus demonstrated was possible.

As my mother ramped up the séances and conjuring and generally caused panic to seep into me like jaundice into an old drunk's sclera, I started to be given advice from my guides on meditations and protective invocations to bring discipline and structure to my mind, and to keep me from being completely swallowed by fear to the point of committing suicide for the thousandth time. And by the way, I can tell you on good authority that suicide does not get you out of any of your problems, but instead, those problems just echo and multiply in your next incarnation. And no, I don't believe in reincarnation; I *know* it happens. And no, reincarnation is not a good thing; it's a real pain in the ass, as my story so far is making evidently clear. Our job is to get off the little wire wheel in the ego cage we've built and become what God has willed for us, which is for us to be with God, like God in every way, and to extend God's Love and create jointly with God.

Anyway, one day when I was maybe about eight or nine years old in that lifetime, and still playing footsie with this devil character, I was leafing through an old first-edition book of engravings my father had gotten that depicted the fall of man from paradise, and there were pictures of the devil, first tempting Eve, then causing all manner of trouble for men through the ages. Just from looking at those illustrations, I could see he was a real asshole. It was then that I started to realize that I wouldn't be able to make a deal or reason with him, since all he seemed to want to do was cause trouble for anyone he encountered. So, it was then that I decided to build a spiritual fortress to protect my family and myself from this nasty little fucker.

The highlight of my mother's dip into witchcraft came one night when her brother and his wife, along with my mother and father and a few others, were gathered around the table, and an Indian spirit took over my uncle's body, bouncing his head off the table to the point of a near concussion. When that happened, my mother decided that hosting these events was perhaps beyond her capabilities as a spiritual conjuror, and she set them aside.

It was about then that I came across a book that showed symbols that offered protection from nefarious spirits — or at least, that's what I thought they were supposed to do. And so, I became a mystic, doing little prayers in front of all the doors and windows in my childhood home, then crawling up on a stool or chair and drawing little markings in chalk at the top center of each opening to keep the evil spirits out. And while I'm sure now that my mother put away her crystal ball and Ouija board because the experience had gotten out of hand with her brother, at the time, I was convinced that I had put a stop to the flow of confused and angry spirits that my mother had invited into our home.

When I think on it now, I can't blame my mother for reaching into the afterlife in the hopes of pulling out some proof that all our consciousness might live on somehow. To a body, death can look pretty convincing. One moment, her loved ones are alive and joking with their family, and the next, they're in a box with cold, painted faces and waxy hands sticking out of wool clothing. All of which leaves an image of eternal distance etched in our minds that's hard to deny from where we're sitting. And in fact, that is the argument the ego uses as a time-honored tradition of proof that bodies are real, and spirits are imagined. Bang, bang! The ego shoots you down. Bang, bang! You hit the ground. Bang, bang! You're dead, and no man of religion or science, save one in all the billions who have lived and died, can breathe life back into a carcass that is past its expiration date. And the one who did breathe life into the dead has been dead himself and mostly quiet for two thousand plus years, and he took that parlor trick with him when he went. That, or the people closest to him, who covered up the path leading to his death sidestep, have done a really good job of keeping it from the rest of us.

Then Epinoia whispered love into my mind. "My sweet child, the difficulty in this story is that you believed all this to be true. Bad angels, ghosts, angry priests, a lost mother, and only Jesus can reclaim life. This makes forgiveness impossible. When we look at a sin and think it real, then forgiveness must be a lie. You cannot pardon the Truth, especially God's Truth, because God doesn't make anything that needs to be forgiven. Forgiveness of your priest is not a matter of looking past what you think is there. It's not an unfounded effort to trick yourself into making an illusion solid and permanent.

"To make the priest, your mother, your father, or yourself guilty is to make it everlasting. We can never get beyond a sin. That's why the stories in religion all make hell eternal. Eternal damnation is used to justify and solidify a dream. If we forgive a sin, we are damning the illusion twice, once by what we think either they or we did, and second by those who offer pardon for the insanity. But real forgiveness offers sanity because it is an acknowledgement that sin is not real. Your forgiveness here is about laughing at how ridiculous it was. A drunk and smoking priest, a mother with a crystal ball, a father complaining about little strips of paper and percentages, and a little kid doing rituals over doorways to protect his family from the ultimate crazy called the devil. A soap opera couldn't be more senseless.

"My beloved, ask yourself, would you accuse yourself of doing all those things? Holding séances, or condemning a child to hell because he copied a sin from another child's breath? We use lies to condemn. We are all One in Truth, so if we accuse another of a sin, we are accusing ourselves of a sin. To perceive forgiveness as it is, we must break the chain we would place upon ourselves. No one is ever condemned to hell alone, and none can ever enter Heaven alone."

Chapter 13.

Do Little Green Men Have a Little Green God?

Epinoia said, "Reincarnation isn't real. None of this is real. Yet we think we've spent many centuries becoming who we think we are on a given planet. Many, many lifetimes — more than we can even imagine. From the idea of our life as a body, it's easy to think that the body is real, and that this is the only one we will ever get. It makes it easier to justify the selfish way we approach each other, rather than the self-fullness we were meant to offer one another. We can fear each other and protect little bits of paper and shiny pieces of metal and plastic because we believe they belong to us, and that other people are not nearly as honest, trustworthy, or generous as we are, and other people will invade our space and take our stuff.

"I imagine you thinking in so many lifetimes, *Hey, spirit girl, take a walk in some slum with a wad of cash hanging out of your pockets and see what happens. Or park your car in the wrong place and forget to lock your doors, and see how that works out for you. Maybe you'll get lucky, but it was only luck that prevailed, not blind trust in other people. The same is true of people; left to their own devices, they will steal our heart and trample it. You must protect your heart, because there are no trustworthy people out there who will tread lightly.*

"You have been mistaken when you believed that you were defending yourself, that you were being attacked, and that those attacks were real. You planned your future around illusions, and then tried your best to control those illusions, but you always failed. You operated based on the idea that you needed to protect yourself and those you loved from what was happening, or worse, what might happen if you didn't put up your guard every moment of every day.

"Every ego world is based on the idea that there is a threat, and there is scarcity. All the laws, the so-called justice, armies, structures, methods, interactions are based on this insane belief: something or someone is out to get you, and it's only a matter of time before they succeed. In that last life, you were running from the devil because a few sentences earned you a sentence of eternal damnation. It was a sin so profoundly horrible that you could never escape it, and in time, the devil would reach up from the darkest regions of the universe, and in a fiery moment of vengeance, you would be swallowed up and tortured.

"The only way this dream works is if the body that you were protecting and that was condemned were weak and could be held in torture. To the priest, your mind was a prisoner to the body, which could be tortured. And so, you planned your life around this idea, this illusion. When you were a woman living in fear of being raped, you planned your days, weeks, and even months around the idea that you were going to be captured.

"But a healed mind doesn't plan. It simply carries out the plans being offered by the Holy Spirit, with great gratitude that the healed mind is no longer a slave to the body it imagined. The only dependence it relies on is its ability to carry out the plan being offered. A healed mind is secure in its knowledge of God's Love and expresses that Love throughout humanity. In this way, the healed mind is the light of the world and brightens every mind it encounters.

"What did your grandfather say in this last lifetime? Something about little green men, wasn't it? The question involved God being universal for every sentient mind. Do you recall? Why little green men? That's funny. Why green? Why little? A bubble from the mouth of a fish is round because it is the most energy-efficient shape. People here look like they do because it's the best way for people to look. On other planets, they look like different people — perhaps green, perhaps red, perhaps transparent. Tell me the story in that mirror as a break from the attacks we've been reviewing."

A glassy mirror stood waiting before a gowned man. This is what I recalled: my grandfather on my father's side once wondered out loud, if there are sentient beings on other planets, would our God be their god? He didn't say it like that. He said something like, "If there are little green men on another planet, is their god green, or is it the same God we have?" I think what he meant was, regardless of whether we worship the same way or not, is God the same for everyone?

That question sat in my mind for many years, and I would contemplate it from time to time. I'd be at a science-fiction movie, and while I imagined other people were thinking about the action, I would be thinking about how they worship and if God was the same for them as it is here on earth. Beyond the space battles and laser blasts, was there a clergy in some temple or church someplace, scaring the shit out of little kids that if they didn't behave, they would find themselves in hell — or in my case, skipping past the warning and getting right to the damnation — and that there is a Caucasian guy with a white robe in the clouds someplace, looking down at them with a magic scorecard, taking notes?

Then I would think, *They look like they're using their spaceships to fly right through the heavens. So, how far out would God have to be, not to get bumped into at some point?* Of course, when I would ask people what they thought, if they didn't think I was completely mad, and if they answered at all, they would say something like, "Well, God is mysterious, and nobody really knows."

Your Bible (I say "your" Bible as though I know you, but what I mean is the Bible most Christians cling to), in the Book of Matthew, says, "Ask and it shall be given you; seek and ye shall find; knock and it shall be opened unto you: For everyone that asketh receiveth; and he that seeketh findeth; and to him that knocketh it shall be opened." There are a lot of interpretations of this passage, as there seem to be for nearly every passage of the Bible, but it seems clear to me. If you ask for the Truth, and if the Truth is what you want more than anything else, you will find the Truth. In my own experience, the Truth, while never changing, can look different depending on your own point of view.

In other words, the more knowledge we have about the Truth and the nature of God, the more clearly we see the Truth for exactly what it is. Further, the more open we are to seeing God's true nature, the more clearly God will present itself to us. Sadly, very few of the people I've met on this planet in this lifetime have been open to seeing the Truth without their own veil covering Its brilliance. I don't mean to be judgmental (even though there isn't any other way to be in life as a body), and I don't know what is in anyone else's mind exactly (even though we all use God's Mind in reality), except that in my own search for the Truth, I have met a precious few who were searching with children's eyes, and who were open to seeing the Truth just as it is, without casting their own judgments to obstruct the reflection of God.

Jesus tells us that we need to unlearn what we think we know so we can "see" the Light of God. We can't see God's Light with our eyes, in our heads. Not because we will go blind, which is total bullshit; and not because God is so awesome that It can't be seen, either. It's because your eyes are of the ego, or of the devil, which makes it impossible to be open to the Light of God. Our eyes see only what the ego projects, not what is real. To see God, we need to use our inner eye — the eye God created when God thought Us into existence. You and I are in God's Mind, as a thought, unchanged, exactly as God intended Us to be. And nothing any of Us do on this plane can change God's Mind (God is stubborn that way). Then we do all this dramatic crap to try to blemish how God must think of us, asking questions that are not really questions, but statements, and then point fingers at each other in the hopes that the god of hate will find someone other than ourselves guilty ... all because we so want to take our egos with us into Heaven.

We're so egotistical that we want to be our separate selves even in Heaven. We want the god of hate to acknowledge us as we are in a body and embrace the craziness we've come to cherish. "If I can't be me, I don't want to go." Maybe I'm good at sports, and I get a real kick out of being good at hitting a ball, or dribbling, or swinging a club, and I just don't want to give that up. Or maybe I'm terrific at business — or maybe I suck at everything, but still, my perspective is so interesting that God surely must be impressed enough to make an exception just for me. Still, maybe God does hate me, in which case, I don't want to go before the god of hate, because he will certainly send me off to a special place in hell. The shit I pulled in this life is enough to make anyone cringe. Ugh ... I still have some doubt, don't I?

Epinoia said, "What I can tell you is that you won't miss any of the thoughts you have. Once you reach Heaven, you will no longer have any doubt. It won't be boring in Heaven. It won't leave you wanting anything. There is nothing on this earth, on this life plane, that you will want to take with you, except Love. Not bargain love; not the love you give to someone because they hit the ball, or danced the dance, or sang the song, or cleaned your shirts, or made your bed. My dear child, the Love I'm trying to share with you is the Love of God, the Love that is your True nature. When I tell you that there is nothing in this world you will want to take with you, I can tell you that in Heaven, you won't even think of any of the things you thought you wanted here. Once you get even a glimpse of the Truth, everything you think you love here in this world will be pain and suffering. It's tragic. Eating is tragic. Golf is suffering. Sex is painful (which explains the faces you all make when you do it). When Jesus says, 'You are not a body, you are free, you are as God created you,' when you first feel it, and then when you come back to your body, your body feels like heavy, wet, dirty overalls. It feels vulnerable and unprotected. It feels fearful and attacked, fussy, like an old beat-up car with exhaust problems and a dead squirrel under the front seat.

"I know you don't want to give up your body. I get it. You've spent countless lifetimes perfecting your ego, and you've invested so much in it, you just can't let it go. Your body is too much to give up, right? All your friends, all your thoughts and ideas, all your special relationships, that next slice of pizza — it's all gone, in an instant. How could God be so cruel? How can he ask so much of you? What kind of sick bastard would create a perfectly complex world, only to tell you through some crazy, condemned person that you can't take your idea of who you are into Heaven, and that you must unlearn all that you have invested in? I'll say it for you, because I've stood on cliffs and in the desert and screamed at God just like you have: 'Fuck you, God!'" And then she giggled at her own statement.

She continued, "To the ego, God is kind of like a mom who insists all her kids play nice. Except that same mom takes it to some crazy extreme and starts babbling on about how she had but one child, and all her kids are that one kid. And at first you think, *Crap, Mom has gone completely batshit bonkers. She doesn't see any of us. She only sees all of us as one person.* But over time, you start to realize that she doesn't see us all as separate, because she has so much love for us that we're all the same to her. Suddenly, she doesn't seem so crazy after all. You begin to see that she even loves the little brother or sister you have that nobody likes — the one that Dad wishes were never born, and that none of your siblings can stand to be around. He's such an arrogant little screw-up, except that Mom, with her rose-colored glasses, loves him, too. And she doesn't just love him; she loves him so much that she wants to *be* him — to extend herself through him, in him, around him. He, like you and your brothers and sisters, is an extension of her. And who am I to tell you this? I'm you. I love you so much that I want to be you, so I guess I'm also your mother.

"You're still listening to me, so I've failed in my last approach to convince you of who you are. If I had won, we would both be together in Heaven — and when I say 'together,' I mean really together, like beyond enmeshed. More together than a Jewish mother and her only child.

"Let me try this another way. You know how when you sit for a long time in one spot, your foot falls asleep, and you try to walk, but you're wobbly because your foot isn't responding, and then it feels all tingly and it hurts? Well, I'm like the tingling in your foot. I'm here to try to wake you up because we're all part of the same mind. We're like a huge piece of cloth, and each of us is one little thread in the cloth, and no one part of the cloth can be awake all by itself."

Then Epinoia said, "Ugh, that's not a good metaphor. We're not cloth, we're thoughts — well, a single thought. And that original thought, God's thought of Love, is ancient. Except it's older and fresher than that, primordial or primeval — and why do these words both start with the letter *P*?

"You'll have to think back to the beginning, back before the big bang. Start going back in your mind until you can't go any farther. The first thought you ever had. Not in this life, not in any life, but your first conscious experience. The moment of first awareness. When I first started looking for the Truth, my mind skipped from lifetime to lifetime, looking for anything I might have missed. Like a silver ray of light traveling from universe to universe, from planet to planet, scraping my mind — our mind — for the longing that pulled me back to the Truth of our origin. Search your mind and see if you can find it. I know it's there. It must be. Even if you are a psychopath who has killed hundreds of people, that longing is there. In fact, it's probably why you killed people in the first place: to cover up that longing.

"We're all afraid at first of our True nature. We're powerful beyond all imagining. The mind we're made from is the

Mind of God. The world we made is a twisted shadow of the Truth, but it's still remarkable. Now if you and I could just take the veil off the world we made, our third eye would open, and we would see, for the first time in such a long time, the pure light of God, and God will take the final step, and we would come to know that We have never left Heaven. We are home.

"We can tell each other ghost stories about demons reaching their creepy hands up from the grave to pull us down into hell, but they are just stories told in fear. God doesn't make stories real. When a child wakes up from a nightmare, you don't encourage them to stay in the dream. You tell them it was just their imagination. Wherever you are, stop for a Holy Instant and allow God to lead you, and see where it takes you. Search, and you will find. Listen, and God will speak to you. And His voice is like the most beautiful music formed from the laughter of angels. His message is of complete security and Love, where attack has no meaning, and your fears all melt. Wait for a moment and listen with all your valuing, and you will remember the original thought of Love."

But can we find perfection in a dream? My most recent visits to Heaven have taught me otherwise. Grace, the perfect Love of God, of which we are all an extension, cannot be altered. Thank God for that, if nothing else.

As I looked around this dream of my grandfather, I was in his kitchen. He had a tall glass of bourbon in front of him and challenged me to arm wrestle. He said, "If I win, the aliens are green. If you win, they're whatever color you think they are."

I won. Turns out they're deep blue with little yellow dots. I never told him that; he asked me how school was going before I got the chance. I told him it was difficult.

Epinoia giggled.

Chapter 14.

What is a Miracle?

Epinoia said, "Have you ever wondered what a miracle really is?"

We were back in the house of mirrors. Like Epinoia had said, many of the mirrors were already gone, and with them, any memory I had of those so-called lives. They had drifted off like a gentle breeze, and the only thing left was a joyful giggle at the change of mind and the moments of pure love. Her question drew my attention to the idea of anything supernatural. Raising of the dead? Here I was, dead, but not dead. Without a body, yet still aware. Just a shadow of the ego that had kept me trapped in a long line of insanity. So, I guessed that couldn't be right, because there didn't seem to be any death in reality.

Walking on water? Turning water into wine? God sending some stone tablets with commandments on them?

I told her that now that she mentioned it, I wasn't sure, exactly. Something supernatural? Reading minds, or some sort of energy healing of the body? Moving mountains? That seemed like a go-to miracle every spiritual being loved to claim: "You'll be able to move mountains with your mind." So, I pleaded, "Tell me."

Epinoia responded, "My beloved, it's a change of mind. Miracles are a great equalization of mindfulness. It flattens ideas in their craziness, making them all the same in untruthfulness. Miracles don't really matter; what matters is where they come from — and they come from the Heart of God. They occur naturally as expressions of God-Love. When they don't occur, something has gone wrong, and the mind is preoccupied with the ego.

"Miracles and miracle workers are habitual, and the miracles happen unconsciously. If you allow your ego to select miracles, they then become unnatural and misguided. They are an extension of Love from one who temporarily has more to one who has less, but only in that moment. Once the miracle is offered and received, both the one who 'gave' and the one who 'received' are both healthier.

"Some believe that miracles are only performed by the enlightened few, as special events to 'prove' that God is real.

Like parlor tricks to impress followers, they turn miracles into magic performed at parties. Instead, miracles — true miracles — are prayerful thoughts that represent a higher level of experience. Miracles bear witness to the absolute Truth. There was a time in one of your life experiences when you thought you were a young girl who had died and come back. Many around you said it was a miracle. Did you believe them? Do you agree with that thought now?

"Real miracles show you what you are, as God created you. They restore a fullness that has slipped from your memory. My beloved, go deeply into your memory, and find the original thought of God. Not what so many think of as original sin, because there is no sin, but that original memory that God placed in every mind at the very beginning. That memory is being shared with everyone you encounter when miracles take place. They restore your mind to its fullness and offer that same fullness to all other minds. Like a chain reaction, or a virus, but in a good way, one loving thought touches on the next, and the next, and so on. The original thought of Love may not even be recognized at first, and its extent may not be realized by everyone it touches. Miracles honor God's creations as they were intended to be." And then she giggled as that memory reached from her mind to my mind. The blessed miracle thought was something I recognized.

"You'll need to find forgiveness for the near-death experience you believed you had. It was another example of being a survivor, and a victim as well. You were never a victim of the world you projected. All those experiences were made up by you and pushed out as a reflection of what was in your mind. Do you recall that 'once upon a time' when you were a little girl on a farm?"

I then slipped into a robed figure in front of a mirror showing a child living on a farm. The farm was small and wet in early spring. The warm breath of summer was just starting to exhale. I was sitting up in my father's lap on his tractor, and we were rolling and bouncing through the muddy fields. It was one of those red tractors with an exhaust pipe at the top with one of those little caps that would bounce open and shut as my father planted his foot on the gas pedal. I made a monochromatic humming sound that jiggled with each bounce, making me giggle. My father laughed at my humming, which made me giggle louder. Perhaps it was my giggling that drew his attention away from the fallen tree stump in the field, or maybe the blended colors, all the same sloppy brown mess. But the little bowed front tires hit the stump, and the tractor gave a mighty lurch, knocking me off my father's lap and under the massive rear tire. The tractor rolled over my little body, pressing the air and much of my blood out of me, leaving me for all intents and purposes dead.

I don't recall my father stopping the tractor or hauling my little lifeless body back to his truck and rushing me to the doctor's office in town. I don't recall the doctor's concerned expression as he looked at the whiteness of my body, held in my father's arms, like a weeping willow tree that had just been cut down, my tiny overalls smeared with mud and my torso flattened.

What I do remember is a whiteness. That, and two people who came to me, a man and a woman. They were older, and I recognized them, but didn't know them. They looked like older versions of my mother, tall, thin, fair-complexioned, and kind. I remember their eyes being deep blue, like the sky in midsummer. They each took a hand and told me that I could go back, or I could go with them. When I asked where we would go, they said, "To the next life." The man picked me up and held me close and whispered in my ear, "The choice has always been yours, my dear child."

He handed me to the woman, and she said softly, "Know that you are loved, and always in a safe place. If you go back, there will be pain, but you will recover and live a long, loving life. If you go with us, you will eventually do the same. Your time isn't now; your time is in the future, and the past. The now will come to you, but not in this life, nor the next."

The feeling of being without a body was fresh, free, without any pain. I was tempted to stay there, but the two people told me that I would get restless and eventually want more. The hungry ghost would emerge in me, and I would cling to a body again.

Then I could hear my father screaming at the doctor in a panic, "Do something, she's dying!"

"Sam, she's already dead. There's nothing I can do to save her. She's gone."

My father: "Try, anything — just try!"

The doctor placed his hands on my little chest and began to press rhythmically, and after few seconds, my little body gasped for air. You know how I told you I was wearing dirty overalls? Imagine you have just woken up in the morning, and the only clothes you have are cold, wet overalls. They are covered in mud, all clingy and ugly. That's what it felt like when I slipped back into that little body. I was down to my underwear and T-shirt, but my body felt heavy, cold, dirty, and wet. That initial feeling wore off over time but being outside of my body and remembering that feeling of freedom cast a shadow of awareness that I was stuck in a physical form, and it was never really comfortable after that.

Both my mother and father told me it was a miracle that I had survived, and I was special because I had come back to life from death. When I told them that I had met two people in "Heaven," they asked who they were. When I described them, my mother dug through her purse at my bedside and pulled out a photo. "Was this who you saw?"

I took the photo and held it in my little hand and stared at the two people in the old black-and-white photo. It was indeed the two people I had met. Without looking up, I said, "These are the people I was with. Who were they?"

And when I looked up, my mother was crying and said, "Those are your grandparents. They died just a few years before you were born."

"Your mom and dad?"

"Yes, sweetheart, my mother and father."

In that lifetime, I was convinced that when we die, we would see our relatives who went before us, and that we would be the ones to greet those who come after us. My miracle experience was proof for so many that there is an afterlife, and it does contain our loved ones. We can go with them if we like and live in the hereafter. My parents took me to church after church to tell my story, and to encourage those followers that if they just believed, their dreams would come true. I felt very special, like I knew something that others only wished they knew. I had experienced something that others could learn from. And I spent the better part of that life going from one group to another, telling anyone who would listen that their family and friends would be in Heaven waiting for them with outstretched arms.

This went on for a time, until the newness faded, and I eventually married and had children in that life. I was a "good Christian" who taught Bible studies, and scolded children who weren't listening to the teachings of that sacred book. I felt it was my duty to tell others about the Lord and Heaven, and our savior Jesus Christ. Over time, I became first a grandmother, and then a great grandmother, and all that time, I took it upon myself to tell others what to think, how to act, and what would get them through the gates of Heaven.

My one grandson was my most troublesome task. He was one of those gay boys, what we called "light in the loafers," and he never did marry. One day, we were all sitting around talking, and he mentioned that he liked other boys, not girls. He said it was just the way he was. I tried my best to explain to him that he was making a very bad choice, and that he should rethink his decision to be a homosexual — that God didn't think much of that direction, and he would eventually end up in hell. But no matter what I told him, he would not listen. I went to my grave years later with a heavy heart that I could not get that boy to listen and change direction. He was stubborn.

After I passed in that life, I found myself at the gates of Heaven, behind a line of people who were either already judged to be the good guys (most of them being Americans and their closest allies — just saying — so that was a nice surprise for my evangelical-leaning personality), and a group who were maybe just a little bit sinful, but not bad enough to be in with the really bad bankers and politicians and the like. Best of all, they all spoke English, which is even better, because being an American, I really didn't like learning foreign languages, and since this was Heaven, English it is, with a slightly Southern accent to make me feel right at home.

After a short wait, I came to the front of the line. I started to make a list of my attributes; that I was a great-grandmother and a Sunday school administrator and had gone to church regularly were all pluses. I did swear once in a while, but only when I stubbed my toe, and only under my breath, and mostly using fake swear words like "golly," "jeepers," and "zippity-do-da," so I was sure God would overlook that small flaw in my past. And I only condemned the people I was sure that God would also take issue with. So, while there was some redemption for me to take part in, to me, it was a little like a third-grade math test that I had studied well for, and with a teacher who loved me like her own daughter.

"So, what's Heaven going to be like for me?" I asked, without any question or doubt in my voice or posture that the gates would soon open to invite me in. Having been to Heaven once before, I felt very sure about what Heaven would be like for me.

St. Peter (or perhaps Paul; it's hard to say who was on duty that day) said, "Aw, you'll love it here, Polly. All your family and friends will come to visit you, and we have some terrific card tournaments, and the food is really fantastic, and not too spicy. Plus, everyone does exactly what you like, exactly when you like, and you're never angry with them, because, well, they are God's little angels, you know. And the best part is, all the people you loved are just up ahead in that wonderful, flower-strewn pasture, and none of the people who ever did you wrong are here. Plus, no foreigners to take your spot! Oh, and before I forget, you will never remember any of the bad people; they have been erased from your memory. By the way, you never have to go poop or pee again, even though you can eat all you want, and never gain an ounce! So, enjoy your afterlife, Holly, and welcome!"

"Where is God at the moment? Will I get to meet him at all? And it's *Molly*. I would think you would know that" I said, trying very hard to keep from being annoyed.

"Well, err, Molly, he is in with the bad people, doing some judgmental-type stuff, so in a little bit, he might stop in and visit with you. But at the moment, all I can get you are a couple of saints. Would you like some saints to stop in and say hello?"

"Oh, no, that's fine. What about Jesus? Can I visit with him at all?" I could not help folding my arms across my chest and looking at my feet. In all my Heavenly prayers, I had visualized God — or at least the regular white Jesus — standing just inside the gates to greet me this time, and I was having trouble hiding my disappointment.

"You see, now I'm starting to wonder, Molly. Did you read the Bible at all? Because I thought it was pretty clear that Jesus is at the right hand of God on Judgment Day, and, well, they're both together at the moment. Now, why don't you run along and visit with your good relatives, and forget the bad ones, and after you get settled, God will have a visitor's liturgy this Sunday, and you can spend time worshiping him then. He really loves it when people worship him. Now run along before we start to think that you don't belong here, Molly."

I walked off into the pasture with my other dead relatives and couldn't help but think that I had always imagined Heaven being more, well, *heavenly*. That time when I was a little kid, it was so much more helpful and loving. I was certain that a feeling like disappointment was out of place in Heaven, but I felt it, and that made me feel a little sadness. At the first flash of sadness, I started to feel angry, and that put a tarnish on my visit with my relatives, who all asked, in unison, what was wrong. What I had failed to realize is that if God can have conflicting emotions, then everyone in Heaven would still have them. We are all either a reflection of God, or God reflects all of us — one or the other, but not both. And if I and the bad people couldn't let go of the idea that God can be angry, sad, or disappointed, or have any other emotion than complete Love and Joy, then Heaven couldn't be heavenly.

Epinoia giggled. "Heavenly confusion! With the ego god, anything is possible. I love this next part of your heavenly dream, because it gave you such a wonderful awareness of the Love of God. You began to rethink the whole life-after-death idea you had been experiencing and preaching."

I remembered back to that experience, and that I started to wonder, what if for the most part you love someone, except for a little problem you have with them? Maybe once a long time ago, you know they had a little fling or stole a little cash while they worked the till at Hobby Lobby, because they had to buy their own birth control pills and just couldn't make that happen on near minimum wage. Or maybe it's worse: your grandson chooses to be gay, like mine did, and he just never got that turned around. He even lied to you and told you he was not gay, because he wanted you to feel more comfortable, but you know he was going off to the gay clubs and doing all that sinful stuff that gay people do. So, in your heart, even though you love him — he is your family, after all — you fear God hates him because God hates gays.

Then, when you get to Heaven, a saintly person tells you that your grandson won't be joining you after he dies; instead, your grandson is going to hell for eternity, and you will never be able to see him again. You know this because your Bible says, "In a similar way, Sodom and Gomorrah and the surrounding towns gave themselves up to sexual immorality and perversion. They serve as an example of those who suffer the punishment of eternal fire." And so, it is written, and so it shall be.

How could I be joyful at that thought? Why didn't it make me feel vindicated? How could I feel a little sadness, guilt, and shame that my family member was in hell and still find joy in heaven? At that realization, I didn't find great joy in knowing that one of my grandchildren was in hell. Then I wondered, how do God and Jesus feel about my grandchild? Do they take great joy in one of their creations suffering? Or do they have sadness in that? Do they feel like I do — sad and lonely? They are God and filled with joy, but still, there is conflict. How can that be?

If they have sadness, they cannot be the True God or Jesus, because both are Love, and there is nothing but great Joy and Love in God. And to say that God is a mystery, so we cannot understand his nature, is to say that God is a separate entity that cannot be known — except that can't be true, because my Bible also says, "So we have come to know and to believe the love that God has for us. God is love, and whoever abides in love abides in God, and God abides in him." So, God, the Truth, and Love are all one and the same, and yet if I feel any sadness, guilt, shame, anger, grief, or any emotion other than joy, I'm in a state that is not Heaven. And if God and Jesus feel sadness, anger, hatred, or anything other than Love, then they must be a lie. This was a terrifying realization for me.

How could anyone believe in a god who would cast judgment on people after they die? Who could believe in a God that could get angry at something a person does? Is God so weak and psychotic that any single person could change God's mind about anything?

All I could think is that I must have misunderstood the Truth about God.

Epinoia said, "This was a tipping point for you. This was the moment when you began to look deeply into your mind to seek for the Truth. Truth be told, I shouldn't say *the* moment, since you had many of these moments when you started to turn away from the ego and look towards the Holy Spirit.

"Our *brother* Jesus tells us that healing is like a sound. He states that healing is completely in your mind, and by 'mind,' he doesn't mean in a brain. Heaven is a feeling of the ego being melted and your identity becoming clear. And the idea of yourself as a body doesn't make any sense there because you are completely healed in spirit. When Jesus says, 'You are not a body, you are free,' he means literally that your body is an illusion and doesn't need protection. It's just a thing, like a table, or a car, or any other thing around you. It's not good or bad; it is a meat puppet that your mind created to dance with the devil.

"See me without the history of what you think you know about me. See yourself for the first time, not as the person you think you are, but as the person God knows you to be. And in that moment, you will see your friends and enemies are all the same. None are special, none are attacking you, none are here to hurt you, and none are doing anything that you have not asked them to do. See the world through the eyes of Christ, and you will see for the first time, and at the same time once again. For you have just forgotten who you are. But not completely — just almost completely. So, uncover the lovely sound of God's True Voice, and the music will gently surround you and penetrate you, removing all that you have made and replacing it with all that you are.

"Sit now with me, in quiet anticipation of the return of our Brother, and wait for Him to lead Us. Ask the Holy Spirit to tell you where you need to be, what you need to say, and to whom. And never again plan with the ego about Heaven or judgment, but instead, allow the Holy Spirit to make those decisions, and let go of all that you think you know. Together, we can enter Heaven, as one. Alone, we cannot go, where together, we can glide on the air of the sweet breath of God. Let God whisper Its gentle Love, calling you back home. There is nothing here that is worth one more of your beautiful thoughts and staying here with the ego is nothing more than a tragic waste of less than a moment, not even a moment, in reality.

"Know that you are loved, no matter what you think you have made up about your life and the people around you. You think you know what you have done, and you think you have taken notes on those around you, but God thinks otherwise. The ego heaven you thought you knew was fake. It was an illusion, so it was not real. Let it go, my beloved. *Let it go.*

"One more bit of knowledge I can share with you: you thought you were right about a lot of things, but there is great gladness in finding out that you really don't know anything. It's okay to be wrong, and it's a joyous occasion that the Holy

Spirit is waiting in silent patience for you to admit that you don't know what anything is for. Even Einstein didn't know what anything was for, and he was pretty smart. So, take a moment with me and let go of everything you're holding onto, and allow the Holy Spirit, or Jesus, or God to lead you. Nothing bad will happen. You won't wind up in hell for all eternity, and you won't be forgotten.

"This much I know for sure: Heaven is not a place for judgment. It is release from the judgment of an insane god made up out of fear. Heaven is not a place where your sins are cleansed and forgiven. It's a place where sin was never real, and where you have been all the while that you thought you were in a body.

"Are you ready for this idea: there isn't any place for a body in Heaven. The idea of a body doesn't fit there. There isn't any place for words, thoughts, ideas, work, anger, sadness, loss, Uncle Tony (if you have an Uncle Tony), or aunts, or parents, or anything other than God. And when your Bible says, "God is Love," that is the only thing that is completely True in that or any Bible. God is simple and completely without conflict.

"Now, I don't want to freak you out, but there isn't any place for you or Jesus in Heaven, either. Hold on before you turn your back on me and start telling me I'm headed straight for hell. Let me explain because Jesus is the one who told me to tell you this. In Heaven, there isn't any room for more than one. There is only the feeling of God and nothing else — not because there is scarcity or lack, but because God is everything, and we are all an extension of God's Love.

"So, what that means is that Jesus, you, your mother and father, your grandparents, your aunts and uncles, your brothers and sisters, people you hate, and people you love are not there in person, because they are there in spirit, and there is only One Spirit we all share. Jesus isn't there as Jesus, because you are Jesus, and so am I. We are all an extension of God, and the feeling is one of inclusion and abundance — but not like abundance on a planet in a body, which means having a lot of money and power. It's a memory of being complete in the abstract embrace of God.

"Having said that, I must admit there is something Jesus and I both need from you. God has offered a gift to all of us, and if we don't all accept the gift, Heaven cannot be entered. Simply put, we cannot enter Heaven alone.

Epinoia continued, "Near death, no death, only death — that's what the ego offers. That instant in that lifetime gave you a clear view of the price we pay to 'be ourselves' and 'live our own life' in separation. When you said you slipped back into that little body, that's not actually true. That's what it feels like — like we're in a body looking out, and all around you was stuff, other people, animals, and on and on. But the opposite is true. Your body in any dream is in your mind.

"Now, my sweet child, sit with that realization and forgiveness for a while. We have more magic mirrors to peer through. The mirrors will be getting darker now. You have been the victim in most of your mirrors so far. But you will need to take on the darker mirrors as well. This is the difficult part. Like the time you were a senator who liked transsexual teenagers. Do you remember that experience? We don't need to go right into that lifetime, but it came to mind for you, so you must be ready for that forgiveness now.

"Rest, my beloved, and when you're ready, let's take another trip together into the dimly lit mirrors and see if we can find forgiveness there as well.

Chapter 15.

Can God Be Angry?

Epinoia came to me like the smell of lilacs on a gentle breeze in spring and carried with her the Love of God into my mind. I wish I could reach out my hand and touch you, and her love would flow from me to you, so you would remember, like I did, the Truth of who you are. If that were to happen, you would never doubt yourself or your value again.

She said, "The ego god of hate casts judgment. Hey, it's his job. If he didn't, there would be chaos, right?

"Ego belief in God brings with it a dilemma. If any thoughts and actions can make God angry, then Heaven and how we get there become imbalanced and unstable. The True experience in Heaven is the opposite of the ego projection of God. God isn't angry or in conflict. There isn't any judgment because there wasn't anything to judge. In the Oneness that is God-Love, the idea of opposites cannot enter healed thoughts. Our awareness is present in an eternal moment, but you or me, as separate people, we're not there. Not because we don't belong there, but because there wasn't any frame of reference for a personality with desires and lust, or any separateness.

"Let's remember the dream you had as a senator, when you imagined the god of death sitting on his golden throne, looking out at all he created and taking credit for all the good stuff, and blaming all the bad stuff on others. He had his angels standing guard, Jesus at his right side, and he brings in all the bad people in chains and casts judgment on them. They all beg him for mercy, but by now he is so angry that he can barely even look at these bad people. He looks down his nose and doesn't even lift a finger, and with a simple thought, all the bad stuff they did is shown on a magic screen on the side of a cloud. The bad people whimper in fear, knowing now for the first time that they were wrong about everything, and that there is a god, and now they must pay for every misdeed they did in life, no matter how or why they did it. God has been watching them and has heard every thought they have ever had, and seen it all, even the quick masturbations in the bathroom that only took a few minutes, which is really embarrassing to some of the bad people.

"They kneel and are genuinely sorry, and they cry out like little children, but they were gay, or they were murderers, or they had sex with someone they shouldn't have, or stole something that didn't belong to them, or drank water from a fountain clearly labeled for 'whites only' when they were not white, or baked a cake for the wrong person, or didn't just die because they were poor, or asked for a handout now and again, which God really could not stand at all. Or worst of all, they were the wrong religion, and now they must pay for their unforgiveable sins. Let's face it: God gave them perfectly good bodies and the bible, and all they wanted to do was do the opposite of what God expected, and so God has only one recourse: eternity in hell, you sinful bastards.

"Oops — God wouldn't use those words (remember, that was one of the very first questions you asked me about cuss words). God would never, ever swear, even though he created swear words, because any time those words are used, God gets a sour stomach and a little vomit boils up into his mouth, and he really hates that vomit flavor; it's so acidic. And it makes him wonder why he ever created swear words or vomit in the first place. He's sure there was a reason, but all he can remember is that he works in mysterious ways, and so we'll have to leave it there. Maybe it was so that people would know the happy, good feelings of not-vomit, but it's still a mystery, and you would never understand it anyway, so stop asking stupid questions. There is judging to be done, and God hasn't got all day.

"One of the bad people is thirsty and asks God for a drink of water, and God looks over at him and sees that the man has parched lips. It takes God a moment to think about the question, because no one has ever asked him anything like that before — especially when they were being judged.

"The ego god says, 'You do know you're being judged, right?' God cannot believe the audacity of the unrepentant sinner kneeling before him. What was he? Yeah, that's right: a senator, married, three kids, and a hypocrite who chased after teenage transsexual hookers. A cocksucker who told the world that men who suck cock would find themselves in hell for all eternity. And here he is, on his knees, asking for water.

"The bad person responds: 'Of course, I get that — but I'm judging you, as well. I've spent my life trying to deny my lust for young transsexuals and could never figure out why you didn't listen to me. I had asked for you to change my mind, to help me fight my desires, and to make me the kind of person you would admire and love. You never helped with any of that, no matter what I did. I even became a senator to try to change our entire society and get rid of those cute young tranny tramps, and you never helped with that, either. As fast as I had them arrested, there seemed to be an endless line of them right behind the ones I had just gotten rid of. So, I thought, 'I'm thirsty,' and I'm in the presence of God himself, in his castle, on my knees, and I can finally actually see you, so maybe if I ask for a drink of water, I'll actually get a direct answer from you. You gave Moses the ability to part the sea, and I'm just asking for a tall, cool glass of the stuff, which to my way of reckoning should not be difficult for you at all. So, can I have a drink of water? Or has my punishment already started?'

"God sits back on his throne and raises an eyebrow. Just a sliver of conflict has slipped into his brain, and he, for less than a nanosecond (which to the brilliant mind of God is forever and then some), runs through that idea. He has heard this man pray for help in changing his mind hundreds of times, yet off he would always go, sticking his dick in the ass of some young boy, many of them as young as eighteen, and once with a boy who was maybe sixteen at the oldest. He knew it was wrong, asked for forgiveness, asked to be changed, but did nothing to hold back his desire. Did he ever pee his pants? That was a desire, too — but no, as far as God can remember, the senator has never peed his pants, except that one time in the airplane when lightning struck the tip of the wing and the plane nearly crashed, and at least a dozen people lost control of their bladders, and one even lost control of her bowel, which isn't a sin, per se, but is really gross.

"The ego god says, 'You had free will. What more did you need?'

"The bad man spits on the ground. 'Fuck free will! Who is free of desire? What I want to know before you send me off to hell to suffer for eternity is, why the fuck didn't you just make me the way you wanted me?'

"Before God can answer, a petite young woman, also on her knees, coughs. She is one of his prettiest creations — dark eyes, black hair that turns blue when the sunlight bounces off it, and lovely olive skin. She is Arab and a virgin.

"God casts his steel-blue eyes on her. 'Is there something you wanted to say?'

"She coughs again and says, 'I'm a bit parched as well. Also — and I don't want to make you angry, Allah, honor be upon you — but why am I here? I'm a virgin.'

"God then projects her short life on the screen, and she sees that she didn't respect her father, didn't listen to her mother, didn't obey her younger brothers, and had serious doubts about there being a god who allowed her to be kept as a slave, especially since she was smarter than any boy or man she had ever met, but wasn't allowed to go to school.

"The little Arab girl says, 'Oh, I see, you weren't kidding about all that. So, now what happens to me?'

"An angel looks down at her and says, 'You're one of the virgins who will service the latest martyr as a sex slave.'

"'But I… Except he killed people… Aren't they supposed to not do that? Isn't killing people worse than not listening to your father and not obeying your brothers? You can't be serious, Allah, all-loving father of life!'

"Then God says unto her, 'I have judged you and made you the sex slave of the martyr Ja'far, as he did what he did in my name, and for that I am grateful. Those infidels needed to die. And by the way, you are supposed to be in his bed in fifteen minutes, so shut up and be gone!'

"Just then, two black angels slither up through the floor, grab the young virgin by the ankles, and drag her down into hell — err, Ja'far's heaven, or her hell, anyway — and she never does get the water she was looking for, nor a solid answer about the whole killing thing being worse than being a little impudent.

"Then the god of the ego says, 'Now, back to you, senator — free will and all that. Don't put your desires on me. That wasn't my fault. That was *your* fault. You chose to be a fag-loving hypocrite, not me.'

"Without answering, Jesus waves his hand, and the senator is dragged off into hell by two new black angels, never noticing the irony of the bad angels being black. His father winks at him and says under his breath, 'That's my boy.' Jesus beams with pride, which is also a sin, but his dad is a little biased with his one and only son, so he lets that little show of pride slip by him.

"God sits back on his throne and says, 'Next!'

"... Remember when I told you that all life is a joke without a punchline? I was being lighthearted with this dream, to soften it a little. But this is the way you remember this moment at the altar of God, right?"

Well, I didn't think it was at all funny, or to be made fun of, but for the most part …

Epinoia continued, "I wasn't making fun of your dream. I was making light of it. It's not a joke — but it is meaningless. This was a very dark lesson for you. The god of hate and anger was cruel, and you spent much time in hell over this instance. You relived it many thousands of times, and searched from one life to the next, each time trying on different psychotic characters, trying to shake this imagined god of the ego.

"To make light of this is to show how little meaning it has. You thought you were a sexual pervert having sex with transsexual prostitutes. For this, you were convinced you needed to be punished, and you spiraled from one so-called crime to the next, always looking for a way to kill the god of the ego.

"The One True God doesn't have a sense of humor. All humor is based on attack, and God is incapable of attack of any kind. Here's an example: A bus full of ugly people had a head-on collision with a truck. When they died, God granted all of them one wish. The first person said, 'I want to be alive and gorgeous.' God snapped his fingers, and it happened. The second person said the same thing, and

God did the same thing. This went on and on throughout the group. God then noticed that the last man in line was laughing hysterically. By the time God got to the last few people, the last man was laughing so hard that he was rolling on the floor. God wondered why the man was laughing so hard. When the man's turn came to be granted his wish, God asked him what he wanted, and the man laughed and said, 'I wish they were all ugly again and back on the bus.'

"To the egoic way of thinking, this is ironic, because the last ego mind wanted to attack the wishes of the other minds on the bus. Also, the ego can judge a person to be beautiful or ugly based on appearances. This is impossible for God because God cannot see a body. God only sees Its own creations, and nothing less. Unless we can lighten our imaginings, we will continue in fear, never to find forgiveness for the crazy things we make up.

"To face our fears, in the deepest and darkest shadows of our minds, we need to see those imaginings for what they are: nothing. You chose the moment of being condemned for sexual misconduct by the ego god. But you have also experienced being a murderer, a thief, a rapist, a sadistic torturer, a terrorist, a slave owner, and even a genocidal maniac, leading armies into battle and killing millions of people. All of this was not sinful; it was mistaken. All of this you would prefer not to take responsibility for. Just using swear words will turn many away from this style of lesson. But turning from the realization that we cannot accuse anyone else of anything that we would not accuse ourselves of will only keep us locked in this nightmare, and the insanity will only continue.

"My beloved, God has a sense of Joy, Happiness, and Love. What you believed you did in those lives never happened. One attack, one event, was not worse than any other. What you are finding forgiveness for is that which never happened."

I had been quiet during her explanation of those experiences. While she spoke, moments of pure evil in the ego way of seeing things flashed through my mind — images of torture, rape, mass killings, events so horrific that they are indescribable. I mentioned that some of these events were so horrible, they made the other events seem insignificant by comparison.

Epinoia giggled. "'By comparison.' That's just silly. There are no levels to suffering, just as there are no levels to miracles. One is not greater or lesser than the next. The moment you are not in the Love of God, you are in hell. It simply doesn't matter how small or large the thought of pain is.

"Egos are always wanting to compare. They say things like, 'You think you've got it bad, let me tell you what happened to me!' Go to any prison in any universe, on any planet, and listen to the inmates. They will all tell you what victims they are. They will compare their crimes to people they see around them and say, 'Look what they did, and all I did was this, or that!', never recognizing that they are making it all up. None of it is real. One mistake is the same as any other mistake. When you were a Bible-thumper, you judged everyone around you. That was a mistake that left you in hell, thinking the world was falling apart.

"You have lived so many lives that they cannot be counted, or even accounted for. And none of them, my sweet child, were real. Like a dog in the yard chasing its tail, you went nowhere, did nothing, and never changed the mind of God, no matter how hard you tried. And when you stand back, it's laughable.

"All so-called sins are based in fear. All attack is fear. Everything you need to find forgiveness for is fear. The strongest, loudest criminal on any planet is just a fearful child screaming for help. The ego takes that fear and builds on it to keep you locked in these crazy dreams. It's a trick the ego mind plays. Then, the ego takes the fear and turns it into loss — a sense of lack, of inequality, or an anticipation of losing. Once the loss is fully established, the ego introduces sadness. It's still fear, but it's in disguise. The sadness is then turned into anger, to lash out at those who have wronged the ego in some way. But it's always God the ego is attacking. When the attack is made, the ego covers the anger with guilt and shame. At the base of all this emotional juggling is fear.

"None of this can be in Heaven, and none of these emotions can be seen by God. If God were to acknowledge these emotions, it would make them real, and the moment that were to happen, God would indeed be dead. It's not young virgins going off to be the sex slave of a martyr, or a murderer going off to do penance for killing, or a misguided woman condemning her grandchild for being a homosexual, or anyone being a sexual pervert. None of those ideas can even be thought of in Heaven. And before you start in on Heaven being different for everyone, that's not true at all, either. There are no good guys and bad guys. There are no Americans, no blacks, no whites, no Asians, and no martyrs, either. And there isn't a special place for Jesus to sit at the right hand of God because the idea of Jesus, and the idea of God as a separate entity, doesn't have any place in Heaven. Heaven is an experience unlike any experience in this illusion, but it is an experience that we have all shared just the same. Best of all, once you remember the Love of God, you will recognize the Love of God. It's something you already know.

"Rest a while, my beautiful extension of Love, and allow these thoughts of forgiveness to seep deeply into your mind. And when you're ready, we can come back to the house of mirrors and see what's left for us to remedy."

And then she giggled.

Chapter 16.

Suicide Isn't Painless, but the Pain Doesn't Last

Suicide is what came to me next. I had returned to the house of magic mirrors and came to a mirror whose reflection I remembered immediately. It was a life that seemed to take place directly after the senator experience. Penance? That life was simply a horrible nightmare. I was a young man who wanted desperately to be a woman. *God has made a terrible mistake,* is what I thought. And I would have done anything to change my body to reflect what was in my mind. All I could think was, *Why, God, did you do this to me?*

This mirror was dark grey — not like twilight, but dull, like drab grey paint on an old car in the desert at dusk, oxidized. The dullness of this mirror seemed to absorb light, pulling it in, like a horde of thirsty tongues cut from sponges. My mind lay flat, without any music, without any love, without any dimension of any kind, except the mirror was feebly attached to an infinite stack of suicidal mirrors. Each was on top of the other, all the same dark grey color.

Yet there was a distant whisper of endearment, and at the corners of the mirror of a million suicides, just a flicker of light. It was Epinoia — not that I could see her, or hear her clearly, but I recognized her. My mind was lost in thought, covered with a thick coat of dismal memories. The thought of digging in a graveyard came to mind. A foggy night in a graveyard next to an abandoned church, and a lone man digging up his master.

Suicide is the most selfish thing an ego can make up. It is hate wrapped in a shit blanket, and it proves that the ego worships death more than anything else. Our ego minds want us to die, but then to cling to the cold, heartless notion that there is an eternity of suffering, to make us special. Each suicide was the same. Life didn't go the way my ego mind had planned, things got worse, loneliness set in, the ego mind started to point fingers, and then I would try to kill the ego to stop the constant nagging and grievances. Each time, whether it was a hanging, slitting my wrists, pulling the trigger on a gun, stepping in front of a vehicle, drowning, or doing something to get someone or something else to kill me, the end result was the same. All the insanity that I thought would leave in death was still there. I still had to face the darkness.

I can point to all the terrible things that happened to me as a transsexual. People around me, my family, people in society, and especially those who had some sort of power in society would try to convince me that I was just a sissy pervert, and that I could never be a real woman. Every day, I was punched, called names, ridiculed, and teased to the point of tears. But as I grew into my teens and started to take estrogen and anti-androgens, that's when my body started to change, and the older men began to approach me. They would tell me how pretty I was and offer me money to have sex with them. I didn't know what to do. The attention other than hatred was desirable, and I wanted to be wanted. So, I would take the money for sex.

But then I would get caught and arrested. The police would sometimes rape me in the back of the police cars, or they would beat me and put me in a cell with older men, who would either beat me or force me to 'take care of them,' while the police guards would watch. Often both would happen in the same night, with the same drunk men. This was very confusing for me, as I would have done what they asked, and then the guilt over their desire for a queer would set in, and they would take their self-hatred out on me.

Judges in the legal system were the worst. They would sit up at their tall desks, looking down at me in my torn skirt, my running mascara, my bruised body, and tell me what a whore I was. They would say that I needed to spend time in a house for young boys, to redirect my proclivities. They would say things like, 'Prostitution is illegal, and homosexuality is a sin,' and then they would cast judgment and punish me. The harshest penalties always came from the judges who had paid me for sex just weeks before. They would act as though they didn't know who I was, but I could tell they did.

As the pain of being cast out of society grew more and more difficult to deal with on my own, that's when the drugs started. Cocaine, smack, dust, and weed. Junk became my favorite. I could feel it seeping into my veins, and the rush of complete calm washing over me, like a wave of warm, synthetic love. It was always the same: the first moments of the warmth, complete distance from the filth and pain my life had become, then the itchy scratchiness, and disrupted sleep, and then the feeling of edginess for more.

As I grew older and less attractive (older men are attracted to youth and do not want a twenty-something whore who has destroyed her body by living on the street and doing too many drugs), it got harder and harder to get drugs, a place to live, or anything to eat. For a few months, I lived under a bridge. I had tried to sleep in a shelter, but being trans and not attractive any longer, there was very little sympathy, and I was never given a bed. After wandering the streets for a few days, I came across an abandoned apartment building and crawled into one of the closets that had an old mattress stuffed in it. Barely able to walk from the lack of food or water, I found an old bed sheet and used all my remaining strength to strip it into a cord. I tossed it over an exposed pipe, tied a noose, stood on an old, creaky chair, tightened it around my neck, kicked out the chair, and hung myself.

You know, it took longer than I would have liked. My neck didn't snap because I didn't fall far enough. I struggled to get loose, but in my weakened condition, it was simply not possible. After what felt like hours, the room became dark, and everything went blank. What I didn't realize is that the sun had gone down. I still had time left to suffer in that body. When death did finally come, it didn't bring with it a release from the pain. The ego just followed me, laying on the guilt and shame as thick and sticky as tar.

Off in the distance, there was a call of Love. It took me millions of suicides to turn from the darkness into the light. We are all called, but so few make the choice to listen. The ego talks first and is very loud. It knows it cannot go to Heaven, and it cannot survive if we choose Heaven. So, it digs in as deeply as possible. The ego mind wants us to suffer; it loves guilt, hatred, shame, and fear. That's how it survives.

In that life, I thought I was a girl in a boy's body, struggling for two and a half decades until I decided to commit suicide.

Looking into that projection mirror was a daunting task. I felt myself being drawn back into that feeling of loneliness and despair. Imagine a shroud of tenebrosity so thick and impenetrable that it feels like a straitjacket made of lead. I was slipping back into that lost feeling of distance from God, until I started to make out Epinoia's voice calling me back.

She said, "Hey there, my beloved. None of this is real. Remember why we're here. It's to find forgiveness, and you crawled out of this insanity many thousands of lifetimes ago. Follow my voice, my beautiful brother. Turn from the darkness and find the light inside of you. Remember who you are. Each of these dreams of darkness was made up by you to cover the light in you with a fantasy so dark that the insanity would last forever. What you forgot and are starting to forget now is that God cannot destroy Itself. The light is in you, not outside of you.

"Truth has come to you because you have called it towards you. This is your choice. I walk beside you, and you know me. God walks with us, and together we can recover from fear and return to Love. When you hold my hand, you hold God's hand, and we are never alone. Did you believe, just for a small moment, that I would leave you? God and I have never left you, my lovely, beautiful child. There is no place to hide in this or any other dream. None of these suicides are real.

"My dear, dear beloved, all deaths in a body are suicide. We chose to be in a dream, in a body, to have drama and find ourselves in pain and misery, and eventually die. This is our choice. God didn't create any of this. God would never make any of this real. It is all a nightmare of our own making. So, every time you lived a life, no matter if it was one that you thought was wonderful and prosperous, or one that was total misery like the transsexual life, they all ended in death by choice. As people in bodies, we believed that it happened to us, that we didn't choose the course of our so-called life. But we did make that choice. To choose death is always the same: it's suicide.

"You are now and have always been the holder of salvation. It is in your powerful hands. At this moment, you don't completely believe that. There is still some work to do, some darkness to forgive and be healed. But we are coming home together from a long and meaningless journey. These expeditions were taken alone and led nowhere. You were searching, but not finding. And yet, you have found your sister in Love, and we will light each other's path home. You cannot enter alone where we can enter together. And with the light of the Holy Spirit, we shine together, extending back into the darkness of a million suicides, making them vanish, and lighting the path to God. The past is gone, my Love, and we have now made room for God's Presence, in which everything is radiant in the light.

"Feel the Love of God wash away the lost dream and forget that it was ever in your beautiful mind — the mind you share with me; the mind you share with God. Feel how powerful you have become by finding the salvation within. You are the light of the world, and you will never forget that again. Once the light has been recovered, it can never be lost.

"Now, my beloved, you are ready to face the final darkness. And together, you and I, with the help of the Holy Spirit, will enlighten the final darkness. We take this last bit of darkness to the Holy Spirit for healing. Nothing will remain that casts a shadow in that beautiful mind. Take a moment and allow the Holy Spirit to cover you with the warmth and the Love of God. And when you're ready, we can take that final journey into the darkest mirrors left in your mind. We will discover that there are no levels to darkness, just as there are no levels to miracles. One is not bigger or more daunting than another. When Jesus said that murder in a mind is the same as murder in a body, it's true. To think it is the same as doing it — not that it needs to be punished, but that it needs to be realized.

"Know that I love you now and will always be with you. Rest in the plateau for a moment, and when you're ready, we'll walk together."

Chapter 17.

The Dark Night of My Soul

My awareness eventually returned to the house of mirror (singular). I call it that now because only one mirror remained. This mirror had a tall, skinny, squirming creature in front of it. It was human in form, of a sort, but scaly, draped in a cloak made from some kind of feathers I'd never seen before. On its head were horns like that of a Triceratops. It was male — at least, I think it was male; it was hard to determine its gender. Its fingers were incredibly long with sharp, razor-like fingernails. I noticed it had more than ten fingers on each hand, and several arms.

My instinct was to turn away, but when I tried to pull my attention anywhere but toward that — what, demon? Savage? Bogeyman? I'm not sure what to call it, this tall, hunched creature standing in front of a single magic mirror, nearly completely cast in shadow — something pulled me back and made me look at it. As I got closer, its details were beyond the imaginable. It was as though there were a million human beings all swarming around like spiders in a nest, each without any purpose except to make up this Asmodeus-like creature. Then it turned toward me, and I felt a fear so deep that it cast me into a panicked anxiety. Its face was long and drawn, and it squirmed like maggots emerging from rotted flesh.

At first, I thought it smiled at me, showing rotted teeth and a snakelike tongue. But it wasn't a smile; it was a look of exasperated anger. It turned back towards the mirror, and I noticed it was using all its fingers to chase a small dot of light around the otherwise blackened mirror. Just a single glimmer of light. Each time it flicked one of its pointy nails against the glass, the light would appear in a different location. This villainous devil would scratch and bang on the screen, trying its best to extinguish the single light, but the harder it tried, the more elusive the light became.

Projected on the mirror was total chaos: armies fighting, totalitarians barking out insane orders, swirls of hurricanes and tornadoes, volcanos erupting, riots, floods, wildfires, constant hatred and racial conflicts, and the destruction of entire planets. The beast was looking to create a world dominated by its shattered and confused will, but all it could do was create insanity. Being made of pure ego, the demon would make up a planet of insanity, only to have it crumble as quickly as it could make a new one to replace the old. One grievance and conflict after another, with never any rest, always searching, never finding.

I called out for Epinoia, and she answered me from afar. I asked if this was me.

"Yes and no, my beloved. Yes, this is pure ego pressing against God and Love, but no — you are the small flicker of light on the glass that the ego cannot destroy. Try as it might, the ego is not capable of turning away from God-Love completely. There is nothing here that can harm you, nothing to fear, in reality."

"But you said at first that it was me," I said. "Is it me? Do I need to go into that mirror? How will I ever survive that insanity? What can I possibly do to find forgiveness in such psychopathic chaos? There may be light in the mirror, that tiny glimmer, but not in the beast standing in front of the projection. This mammoth demon offers not the least bit of love of any kind. It is beyond redemption. Can God have an opposite? Is it possible that there is a place that God cannot reach? Is there a mind that the Holy Spirit cannot bring back to the Love of God? I thought the Love of God was all-powerful, but seeing this, I have to say, I may have misjudged the power of the devil."

Epinoia said, "My True Love, only what God created is real. It has no beginning and no end. It is not restricted by time; it is eternal. God has no opposite. What you are seeing here is the basis of the ego world, which is the world of perception. Perception is a level of awareness based on senses that are covered in a veil of uncertainty. The Love of God cannot be threatened, and none of this insanity truly exists, and this sacred knowledge is what the peace of God rests on.

"From perception comes the ego's world, which is ephemeral, and from knowledge comes the world created by God. The egomaniac here tries to destroy the Love of God because it is frightened. But no matter what it does, the Love of God cannot be destroyed. God's Will and your will are one and the same. God placed your will as your original idea. You, my beloved, are an idea, like God in every respect. And like God, you can give yourself completely to the Light of God. It is a simple choice. Once that choice is made, the monster under the bed — or in this case, in front of the darkened mirror — will disappear.

"You will not go into this final mirror alone. In minds, together, we can share the idea of Love and bring home the millions and millions of lost souls. I will join you in the idea of peace, and together we will pass through the mirror, find the tiny speck of light, and transform the insanity back to reality. This is a choice we will make.

"The creature you see is the dictator you had become over many lifetimes. You wanted control, so you built worlds and tried to bend them to your will. You made up lies and forced those around you to offer their perfect loyalty to your lunacy. To you, in this nightmare, they were all meat puppets, not brothers and sisters, but objects to be controlled and do your bidding. When they disobeyed, you cast judgment and tossed them aside like trash into a bin. It was, in fact, your greatest attempt to kill God and take God's place, to replace God with the unholy will of the ego, the god of hate, mistrust, confusion, conflict, and sin."

"But it never worked, did it?"

"No, it never worked. When you're ready, you will find forgiveness for all these insane attempts at making a world that would reflect the will of the ego and not of God."

As I turned to the dark creature in front of the mirror, a thought came to me, a meditation I had recited over and over again in my last life in a body: "God, give me Your blessing, so I can see this with the eyes of Christ and find perfect sinlessness."

Epinoia said, "You never have to do this. The choice has never been between dreams. All these so called lost souls aren't real. No soul can ever be truly lost. The real choice is if you would prefer to live in dreams or awaken from those dreams. The dreams you think you like will hold you down in a prison of your own making, just as much as the dreams like these that you don't like. They are all the same. Every dream is a dream of fear, no matter what form it seems to take on for you. Call it a happy dream of prosperity, or a nightmare of scarcity; it doesn't matter which. Only that you are choosing to dream rather than awaken."

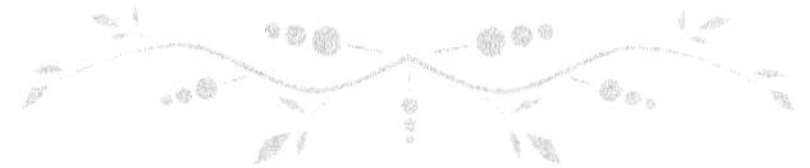

You know what it's like to have to sneeze, and at the last minute, it passes without relief? Or you are hungry for a nice hot meal, but you don't have anything to eat other than a small piece of bread that leaves you simply wanting more? Or maybe you practiced for a test in school, and none of what you studied is asked, but instead, the questions don't make any sense? Multiply those feelings by a trillion in frustration, and that's what this moment felt like.

In the next moment, I was a man in an overweight body in a large office. I was the commander in chief. I was the supreme leader, and I had gotten that position by lying, cheating, stealing, and killing — and then denying all of it.

It was ugly. I simply don't know how else to describe it. I sat at the head of a large oak table with both men and women seated before me, waiting for my direction. Each was loyal only to me. They were all my slaves and would do nearly anything I asked. And that "nearly" part, the glimmer of lack that there were things even they would not do for me, made me angry.

Epinoia said, "Remember when I told you if you could feel the fear in its deepest form, you would completely freak out? This is that point. This is the deepest level of anger, hatred, and at the base of it, fear in its purest expression. Depression, attack, assault, and humiliation are the themes of every dream, because they all come from this deep fear."

Next, I was an old man who had sexually molested his granddaughter. I was defending what I had done to my wife, who was looking at me with the deepest disgust I had ever seen. I was telling her that the child had known exactly what she wanted. I was only doing what she asked for; it wasn't my fault.

Epinoia said, "Maybe sex, or a good meal, or winning a contest can offer a thin veil over the total depression that the ego mind is locked into — but only for a moment. Then the depression returns, even deeper than before. Look within. When we look outside ourselves for what we are, it implies that we are not whole, that we are lacking in some way. Each of the parts of this penumbra to life casts a shadow over the real you — the You that God created, and which you still are."

Then I was a woman who had done everything she could to humiliate another woman at work. I was frightened she might take my place, that my job was in jeopardy, and I needed her to suffer. I did everything I could to make her look bad in the eyes of those around me.

Epinoia said, "The image you see, the monster portrayed here, is of your own desire. You chose your own insanity because it only shows you what you wish. Your idols will only do what you would have them do. This feathery creature is only here because you put it here. The power this creature seeks is the power you would have all to yourself. My beloved, you simply need to wake up from the terrible nightmare."

More images flashed by of lifetimes where I was as horrible as any human could imagine. Epinoia spoke: "These so-called lives flashed from one to the next, each bringing shame, guilt, fear, anger, hatred, and sadness.

"Even forgiveness is an illusion because it is forgiving what is not real. When we forgive — even this giant hellion — we are looking past what isn't real to find what is real. Watch closely as the tentacles reach for the tiny drop of light. Each time it tries to extinguish the light, the light moves. But there is a pattern to the movements. Its ability is limited, so the creature moves in simple patterns that the Holy Spirit can easily avoid. Like a crazy dance, the beast makes the same mistakes over and over again.

"But even in this darkened collection, there is no sin. If there were sin, this would all be real, and eternal, and unforgivable. So many of the moments locked into this reel of horror are victims, holding onto their hatred for those they believe have harmed them. Maybe they were raped, or murdered, or were the victims of theft, or betrayal. The laws of sin require a victim, and so this lord of darkness is filled with victims. Victimizers and victims are one and the same. Be grateful to this image because it is your savior.

"In this moment, the only moment there is, you need to decide how much you are willing to forgive your brothers and sisters. How much do you want peace instead of the dream of hatred and fear? Search your memory, my cherished brother, for the place in you where this entire world has been forgotten and never existed. There is a place in that beautiful mind we share where there was never any sin, and illusions were never imagined. It is the original thought of the Love of God, and it is there for every being that you have ever been.

"This shadow figure of attack can become your brother, giving you a chance to help it turn sadness and suffering to joy in its place. Love is more powerful than hate. Love can overcome any fear. You, my dear, are holy beyond your own imagining. At this moment, while the ghost of illusions still remains, you do not believe you deserve the Love that God is offering. What you look upon as ugly, dark, creepy, and a desolate disaster is, in reality, just a shadow cast over the Love of God.

"At this moment, you look upon this monster and find fear. But this I can assure you: God doesn't see a body, or an attack, or desperation. God has never seen a body. God didn't create a body, or a disaster, or an earthquake, or a murderer, or any other insane, egotistical idea. The moment you fell into a deep sleep of hatred and separation from God, God whispered the Holy Spirit into your beautiful mind to correct the mistake you made, and to wait patiently for you to listen, hear, and follow. All of us are called — even those you think of as truly evil. All of us are called. But so few actually listen. Every flash of insanity you have experienced in this moment, each carries that glimmer of the Light of God.

"You are just starting to listen, and this next step will require you to listen to the Love of the Holy Spirit to lift the veil of shadows, and awaken from the dream, and see past the lies. Open your mind, my beloved, and listen to the Holy Spirit. I am here for you, my sweet, sweet child, and pay close attention; you're almost there."

And then she giggled.

Chapter 18.

I'm So, Not in the Mood

You know what? That giggle didn't help at all. Instead, it sent me into a tantrum. I was simply not ready to listen to Epinoia's giggles, or how this was all "my salvation waiting to happen." Anger started to boil in my mind. Imagine an eighty-year-old overweight man who has been living in a hospital for over a year, being kept alive on medicine alone. He's just lying there, getting a sponge bath once a week, never eating, so they stopped brushing his teeth, and for the past several months, he hasn't opened an eye. Then one day, the nurse suddenly lowers her face near him to whisper something comforting in his ear, and he exhales his last breath just as the nurse puts her nose inches from his mouth. What comes out of him is stale, pent-up decay that is horrendous. It's like his guts had been slowly rotting for a decade in a small closet, and at the exact moment the nurse decided to take a breath, the door was opened, and the stench rushed out like high school linebackers hitting the locker room after a long, hot afternoon workout. Think of that, and you'll get an idea of what my anger felt like.

Enraged? Wildly infuriated? There simply aren't any words to describe the feeling of anger I had at the sound of her giggle. I took it personally. Again, words fail the rage I felt, but I'll do my best to describe what came to mind at that moment and the childish tantrum I experienced, because it may help you identify with those feelings. It's not like I'm the only mind to have these thoughts. We're all completely bound by the mental picture of the world we have projected. We might think that our experiences are unique in some way. But I can assure you, hell is hell. There are absolutely no levels to insanity. We can point to a serial killer and say, "He's so much more horrible than I ever was." Then we can point to a political leader who starts a war and kills millions of people and say that person is even worse. Or a businessman who makes an utter fortune by taking advantage of poor people who can barely make a living, and say, "No, that's worse yet." Or a scientist who experiments on people without their consent, and on and on and on. The anger I felt then is no different than the anger built up in you.

These are all stories used to attack anyone else and make believe it's not us, telling ourselves we would never do anything like that. And in that moment — the moment Epinoia giggled — my mind snapped. Seeing the horror in front of me with this huge, ugly beast and having her giggle like it was nothing was more than I could fathom in that moment. While I was thinking about how to fix the world portrayed in the mirror in front of me, here she was giggling at how insane it was, and how none of it mattered in the least, and actually telling me it is all a joke, and why didn't I see the nonsense being portrayed? It was like her giggle was telling me that I simply didn't get it and had forgotten what a punch line even is.

My focus was on where to start to change the world once and for all. There was so much crazy, it was overwhelming. In my mind, I started to scream, *How can God let any of this happen? What am I supposed to do to change any of this and prevent it from happening again? Where is God in all of this? Where do I start? How do I find that little fleck of light in all this shadow and darkness?* Then my thoughts changed to how I could possibly see any of this differently. In my mind, I screamed at the Holy Spirit, *Show me! How do I see this all differently? How can you allow this to go on and on and on?*

This rage inside me made the monster in front of the mirror move faster and faster. It started to flick its pointy nails with blinding speed, chasing the little speck of light around and around, never able to eliminate the light, but instead making it into light trails. At one point, the crazed monster became just a blur. There wasn't any form at all, but instead a numb shadow, its entire body moving, and yet completely motionless. And then it started to look like it was moving backwards. You know how a wheel on a car can rotate so fast that it eventually looks like it's standing still, and then it seems to change directions? "Reverse-rotation effect" I think it's called. And the egotistical voice in my head started to scream for Epinoia to tell me what to do. I remember saying over and over, "Epinoia, what should I do?", until finally my ego mind lost its words altogether, and my awareness was like a crackling buzz, or a loud, completely insane nocturnal groan. This catachresis went on for what seemed like an eternity.

At one point, I noticed a couple things. First, the blur of the monster was actually motionless, and second, there seemed to be two awarenesses in my mind at the same time. There was the childish crazy person, screaming for Epinoia to "come here this instant and tell me what I'm supposed to do!", and there was an awareness that wasn't involved at all in what was happening in the nightmare. It was as though there were another calm and peaceful mind that simply wasn't interested in anything the blurry monster had to offer, and wasn't screaming for help, either.

It wasn't schizophrenia. There weren't two minds. Instead, there was a true mind and a false mind — and they weren't fighting with each other, either. One was completely calm, waiting patiently for the tantrum to wear itself out, and the other was stomping and crying and simply insane. After a while, my calm mind started to see how ridiculously the crazy mind was behaving. As that happened, the awful moan started to fade, until it finally went silent. Sort of like how a baby stops crying when its mother's nipple is placed in its mouth: a cry, then a few hiccups, a pleasurable sigh, and finally, silence.

In the silence, I heard Epinoia say, "At the base of your anger is fear. What was the fear in looking at the core of insanity? Anger is always a cover for fear. We identify the anger and acknowledge it, but then we go a little deeper and find the fear the anger is covering up."

My egomaniacal fear was simply that nobody cared what was happening. That the wars and attacks were indeed real, and all-encompassing. That I would get pulled into the attacks again and be lost in the battle. I felt that my soul was on the line. I didn't trust that God cared enough to find a solution to the specific personal problems I was seeing in front of me. When I asked if there was another way to look at the world I was seeing, I got no response. My fear was that I was alone in the universe, and that God no longer cared.

My ego mind has never seen an example of God working for the betterment of the world. God has never stopped a tornado from destroying a trailer park. God has never stepped in and told the crazy mass killer to put the gun down. And all the ego world had ever offered was its free will, and that God will punish those who do wrong, and that God is mysterious. My fear in that moment was that God isn't true, or that I didn't deserve God's love. The fear was of being abandoned by God, and that there is a place God could send me that was worse than the experiences I was already having.

That fear lit the fuse to the atomic bomb that turned to anger and hatred. I needed a way to measure myself in the nightmare, to show God that I was at least better than so many others. Maybe someplace in the middle? I had lost the forgiveness I had found with the work we had done together, and my fear was that I would tumble back into the world of grievances and hatred.

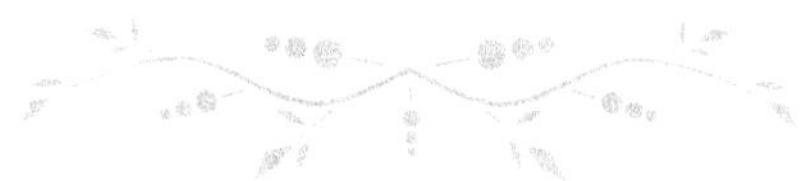

Epinoia said, "Once the fear and anger are acknowledged, the next step is to find your loss. If you had had a face during your tantrum, you would have been crying. With all sadness, there is a sense of loss. Express what that was for your mind in that moment."

Depression, sorrow, unhappiness, and gloom were blossoming from the idea that I didn't matter enough to God for God to speak to me clearly. My loss was that of a sense of true connection to God. In my lifetimes, I had experienced moments, just brief glimpses of the Love of God, but they were fleeting. Most of my time was spent in misery and sadness, always searching for something that was just out of reach. My thoughts led to wondering, *What if the god of hate is real, and I'm a bad person, and hell is where I'm headed?* My loss was that of a sense of trust in God.

So often, books, gurus, preachers, and even my own inner voice would tell me that I was simply not calm enough to hear God — that God was not avoiding me, but I was avoiding God by allowing my mind to wander off and bounce around like a squirrel on cocaine. And my thought about that was how that didn't make sense at all to me. Why would God, of all beings, not find a way to lead that didn't depend on some special connection, or some meditation, or some secret handshake? The gurus would always say, "If you're in hell, you've made the wrong choice, so choose again," or "When you ask for help, why don't you take the advice that is being offered?" And my thought was always the same: *I honestly want to be connected with God, but I find God to be elusive. Listen for God? God is silent, and I cannot hear what is silent. Listen without my ears? Then how do I know what God is saying?*

"Before we can be healed, we must truly want to be healed" is a bullshit statement in the moment of a tantrum. In that moment, I didn't feel as though I had chosen scarcity of love. So many lifetimes, I had wanted more, only to receive less. Abundance in one form or another never seemed to materialize, and when it did, it was only momentary, never lasting. What do I really want? How do I know what I really want? How do I stay focused on what I really want? I don't know what's good for me. God will provide, so only focus on what's important. All of these thoughts have always led me to the same hesitation: what do I do now? And can I trust God to provide? The image of the beast mirror has always been an example of scarcity and mistrust, and God has always been quiet to the point of absence.

When I would ask for guidance, the answer always seemed to be that I was simply not asking the right questions, and that my own mistrust was leading to experiences of scarcity. But how do we place our trust in a god that is either silent or insane? Loss? At the core, love was the loss I felt — the loss of life, of community, of abundance, of prosperity, and yes, mostly of the Love of God. The loss I felt was that of feeling close to God, in line with God's Love. It was emptiness on a level that is indescribable — cold, distant, and alone, unworthy of anything God might offer, and terrified that God would agree that I was unworthy.

Worst of all, I wanted to blame others. I wanted God to punish those who had done me wrong. I wanted God to create a place where anyone who had harmed me would experience my pain, feel my loss, and finally understand the horrible things they had done to me. My loss was that of a sense of security that I was loved, and that God would blame me and not others, and I would go directly to hell.

Wrapped in sorrow, my loss draped over me like a cold, wet woolen blanket.

Epinoia then said, "What about your responsibility? This can be difficult for anyone. We like to think that things happened to us, that we are the victim and not the victimizer. The ego is always looking for someone else to blame for anything that "happens to us." Focus your mind on what you might take responsibility for, but when you do, do not judge yourself. We're not looking for blame, we're looking for causality. And never forget your responsibility to anyone you may have encountered in any lifetime; your responsibility to them is the same responsibility you have to yourself, being that we are one and the same."

This is my responsibility, because when I have really accepted it, I can also accept the atonement for myself. What other choice could I make? In so many lifetimes, I had thought that when I met someone else, they were separate from me; they were another person. Having made the choice to take responsibility for accepting the atonement, I now know that my encounters were all Holy Encounters, because we were all extensions of the Love of God.

God has never willed anyone to suffer. God's Power and Glory are everywhere, and I cannot be excluded from God's Love. The scarcity I felt was my own decision. Ugh, it's painful to say that for the first time! But admittedly, through God's Love and Power, all my own mistakes can be undone. What I thought of as sinful were simply mistakes, and mistakes can be corrected. So, the idea of "choose again" now makes perfect sense. Acknowledge the mistake, ask the Holy Spirit for guidance, and choose again with the Holy Spirit. And this is my responsibility: to accept God's Love for me, to change my mind about my worthiness and realize I am holy. I am a child of God. All revelation, all healing is within my own power to choose God rather than the ego.

My responsibility is to extend God-Love to all I encounter. That is how we co-create with God. The correction and the release from fear is solely my responsibility. When I would ask God to release me from fear, I was saying to God that God had created the fear, that all the troubles I seemed to be facing were of God's making and not my own. It wasn't until I asked for help with the conditions that brought the fear about that I got the answer I was looking for. Fear is always a result of wanting to be separate — to be exclusive, better than, special. I had allowed my mind to wander and was too passive about what my ego mind was up to. I never questioned its planning and conditioning.

My only responsibility is to ask God about any choice I am about to make, and to know for certain that my choice is in accordance with God's plan for salvation. Only when I am sure of that connection is that choice the correct choice. And I will know I made the right choice because there will never be any fear. Fear is always a strain between what my ego wants and what is True because it causes conflict with God's Love. My responsibility is to find the unified goal and be in alignment with God.

Grace comes through making decisions with God. Responsibility is deciding to do what will bring only good to everyone. And how do I know this? I ask God by saying to the Holy Spirit, "Decide this for me." And it is done. There is a deep responsibility I owe to myself — a responsibility I have learned through these experiences. It was difficult at first, but I have come to see the Love in Its Truth. It is a tribute to my own power. It is simply this: every decision I make stems from what I think I am. It represents the value I have placed on myself. I was content with so little, when God is offering me so much more — everything, in fact. But I'm not little. My function is the salvation of all I encounter. I am the light of the world. No, it's beyond any world. I am the Light of God, as that is God's gift to Me, through my Creation. My responsibility is to share that Light with everyone I encounter.

When I slowed down, Epinoia said, "Take a moment and think about guilt. In Heaven, with God, there isn't any guilt. But the ego mind is dependent on guilt. The ego looks to judge, to find sin, and from sin springs the guilty, like hungry wolves attacking a wounded elk. You have seen yourself as guilty of many crimes. It's time to find true forgiveness, because only through forgiveness can we shed the guilt we suffer."

Guilt comes from the belief that we have attacked God, the most serious crime of all, for which we need to be punished. Our actions, our thoughts, our very being, my very being has been an attack on God. I have been guilty of believing that God is angry with me for my original sin of being born outside of paradise. Guilty of thinking the wrong thoughts or having the wrong sex (which is *any* sex). Eating the wrong foods. Saying the wrong words. Killing in my mind or in my body is all the same, and I have been guilty of it all. The guilt I carried (past tense on purpose here) was that I believed I could be separate from God, that I could separate from God's Mind and become something different, special, and better by comparison.

In so many lifetimes, I made decisions with the ego rather than with God, turning my back on the map that God had clearly laid out for my return to Heaven. My ego self-delusion was based on guilt, and it used that guilt to remain in fear — fear of life, fear of death, fear of God, fear of my brothers and sisters, fear of myself. I lived countless lifetimes without any trust in anyone or anything. Most of all, I have been guilty of not trusting the Holy Spirit, often proclaiming myself to be an atheist, because in the ego world, it only made sense that there could be no God.

Guilt was the result of unnatural thinking. Thinking — that's funny. The ego thinks; God doesn't think. What brought on guilt in my mind were grievances, which always turn into guilt in some way. The work we have done with forgiveness has released those grievances and eliminated the guilt carried by the mind I share with God. Actions like stealing would bring on guilt, until I started to project that guilt onto others as a sociopathic remedy, telling myself that "others" should not have left their "belongings" unattended and within reach. Or that it wasn't fair that "others" had so much more than me, and I was "just making things more equal."

Ugh, so much guilt! I often (always?) confused God and guilt because I didn't realize the strength of my own thoughts. I would actually deny my own strength, offered by God, and would project an ego mind that portrayed weakness. I would think of myself as a sinner and would then become a sinner and portray sinfulness — that is, until I understood that freedom and salvation are one, that salvation and guilt are separate, and not together. When I was a preacher — huh, how many times was I a preacher of the god of hate? Many, many times, I was an ego preacher and would tell the story of hate, death, sin, and guilt as the path to salvation. But it was all a prison, not salvation. The words I used from the thoughts I possessed became the bars, and the cell became a temporary home, even though the doors to my prison were always open. I was always free to walk out of the prison cell I had made with my own thoughts, but I chose to stay locked away, fearful that God was ready to strike and send me and my parishioners straight to hell.

A murderer is what I was. It is what all of us are who take on the ego mindset and believe we are bodies. The entire world was founded on attack, and attack is always destructive. The purpose of attack never changes; it is always a form of murder at its core. Whether in thought or in action, murder is what the ego offers, and with it comes massive guilt and frantic fear. We attack, we kill, so therefore we must be punished to "bring justice" to what we have made. We may smile as we attack, and say that what we offer is protection, justice, and fairness, but the smiles will always fail, and the horrific awareness of the purpose of attack will surface once again and become a nightmare. It is simply impossible to think of murder and not suffer the guilt those thoughts inevitably bring on. The intent of the god of hate is always death. It is always guilt. And at the core of death lie guilt and shame, and at the basis of all murderous intent is fear. It is always a god that cannot be trusted because it is a god that is whimsical and unpredictable. It is all based on a god that can be made angry, a god that is weak and thrives on sacrifice.

As I paused, Epinoia said, "You mentioned shame. Tell me more about shame and the difference between shame and guilt."

To start, for me, it entails doubt — the doubt about the outcome of the healing process that God has laid out for me. It was based on the fear of failure due to my own inadequacy — that my weakness would be seen, and brought to the forefront, and my true identity as an imposter would be discovered. Shame, for me, relates to unworthiness. Where guilt is private, shame is public.

For so many lifetimes, I wanted to be special, and my own specialness was dependent on those who were "worse" than me. I would attack and gloat about my imagined "victory" over those who were "weaker" than me in any given moment. My specialness was a triumph, and my victory in that moment was built on the shame and defeat of anyone weaker than me. Except that was fleeting, as I would eventually lose my own foothold and land in defeat and shame in support of another's victory. On and on this would go, life after life, encounter after encounter.

Often, I would allow some dreams and illusions to stay in reserve, dwindling in the shadows of my mind, protected from the Light of God. My thinking was that these events or actions were too shameful to be healed. Perhaps they were things that I thought were done to me, like being raped or murdered. Other times, it would be things that I had done, like rape or murder. Never once did I think, *Is this something I would prefer to hold onto rather than being in Heaven with God?* At the "time," I didn't think that was a decision I could make, that I could simply change my mind and choose again. It never occurred to me to ask the Holy Spirit to help me see those nightmares differently and find forgiveness. What was so, so simple was nearly impossible for me when I was deeply asleep, and the shame of being "found out" seemed overwhelming.

Guilt, shame, sickness, and attack can only happen when minds agree that there is a separation. It is a joint decision. The true miracle is the change of mind that takes place between minds. Miracles are illusions as well because they are not real, in that they are not necessary in Heaven, only in hell. The moment my mind opened up to forgiveness was the Holy Instant that my mind became quiet, and I could hear God more clearly.

What came to mind in that instant was a lifetime far in what would be the future of my last lifetime, but on the same planet. When Epinoia said time has no meaning, God affirmed that when the glimpse came to me of this future lifetime.

Chapter 19.

The Final Battle
(Attack is Never Justified)

Epinoia said, "Let's look at the final tribute to the ego, and the final battle for your lovely mind. One last darkened mirror, and one last stand for the ego to win over Truth."

What I witnessed were troops shooting people, and victims running in fear. The ground was dusty, the trees barren, and everything was exhausted. Complete chaos, random attacks, and nothing made any sense. Scarcity, people running and screaming. In the distance, there was a dried-up river between a city and what looked as though it was once a farm. At least, I think it had been a farm, but it was a desert in that moment. Nobody noticed the man in black across the empty riverbed, watching everyone attack each another.

Across the dusty and vacant tributary, on what looked like a moisture-less farm, was this man dressed all in black, grinning at the mayhem. His pale skin glimmered in the hot sun, a stark contrast to the black shirt and pants he wore. He had black boots and a black hat, but he didn't sweat in the stifling heat. He would flicker his fingers from time to time, as if keeping the beat to music, but no music could be heard. His eyes were like dark pearls, but they didn't shine; they were dull and jaundiced.

What appeared to be a former farmer walked up to the man dressed in black and inquired what he wanted. The farmer wasn't old, but weathered, worn down, so he looked beyond his years. He stood next to the man in black and looked at the dirt at his feet, stirring his shit-kicker boots, causing a miniature gale of dust to spin in front of him and then drift off. The farmer said, "If yer lookin' fer anything to grow here, it won't. God hasn't blessed us with any rain in nearly a decade. I got a little crop of lima beans a few years back, but nothin' since. God has forgotten about us here in the Midwest."

The man in black's face turned to a frown, but he didn't look at the farmer when he said, "You think God gives a shit about your fucking weather? Then you're praying to the wrong god." With that, the man in black pulled a gun from his pocket and shot the farmer in the head, splattering blood on the dusty ground. He did all of this without turning his eyes away from the protest taking place less than a few miles away, and he said to no one, "I hate people who think God has anything to do with any of this. Fucking stupid people deserve to die — every single one of them. Stupid fucks. I am God's word here. It is through me that you reach prosperity; you pray to me or pray to no one, motherfuckers."

Seconds later, a stream of black SUVs ground their way up the dusty road next to the man in black, creating a small dust devil in their wake. A dozen men in military gear stepped out, but the man in black waved them off. They stood at attention, waiting for his orders.

But what caught the man in black's attention was a woman in a flowing gown across the scab of a river, walking calmly through the chaos. Wherever she walked, the insanity was interrupted, and crowds of both police and protesters stopped and just watched her. The trees where she walked blossomed, the grass sprung to life, and the sky lost its haze and became clear, like a fifties painting of a summer afternoon. She turned towards the man in black and started across the river, and as she crossed, the river began to flow behind her. I won't describe her to you, because to do that would be a blemish on her perfection. She didn't have a race, a skin color, or a shape that could be defined, but she was perfect beauty and grace. The look on her face was warm, loving, the epitome of peace and generosity. She represented the light of the world.

The dusty veil that covered the world around her dissipated wherever she turned her gaze. The light that shone in her could not be seen by the ego mind, but the closer she came to anyone she encountered, they were suddenly aware, and their memory of the ancient feeling of peace came back to life.

You know, it has always been there, in all of us, just waiting to be looked upon — not with our body's eyes, but with the Eyes of Christ. Before witnessing this presentation by God, I had always thought of Christ as Jesus's last name, or something that could not be known by a mere human on a planet, always in fear and attacking in insane judgment everyone around me. But what I understood in this moment is that Christ is us, in our perfect form. God created us in God's image, not as bodies, not as creatures that live a short while and then die, but as spiritual extensions of Its great Love. Perfect Love can only create Perfect Love. Anything else isn't possible. To be a person in a body is to judge. My goal as a person in a body wasn't to stop judging, but to recognize that I was judging, and to take those judgments and offer them to the Holy Spirit for correction. To say, "I know I'm judging, Holy Spirit. Help me see my judgment for what it is and help me see this differently."

I tell you — and this is important — that seeing differently isn't to see with the body's eyes in a way that is different. Instead, it's to see with the Eyes of Christ, to see the Love of God in everything. My path, the path I had wanted, the plans I had made countless times were all wrong. And there was great happiness in finding out just how wrong I was.

As I describe the world the flowing woman created as she gently walked across the plains of the Midwest, you may be imagining a lush, green space with beautiful trees, birds, grass, flowers, and all that. And it's okay to imagine that. But that's not what it looked like. It was different than that. It cannot be described in words but know that you will recognize its beauty when you see it. You will know her, and you will know the path she walks, and you will know the home she leads you to. You have been there and are there still. As I watched her gently stride across the plains, time seemed to stop, and the man in black, just for a moment, was caught dumbfounded. She brought with her true reality, where the man in black projected unreality, insanity, and attack.

Her reality was accepted, always being offered. The only difference in her from you or me is that she said yes to God's Love completely. Her only "threat," if you can call it that, was against the illusion offered by the man in black. He called all his insanity to the forefront in his last stand of defiance, in a silly effort to hold onto a power that was powerless, to stave off what he perceived as a loss of specialness and control. The man in black looked for belief where knowledge was being offered.

What we fear, and what the man in black was fearful of, is the most insane thing you could ever be fearful of: We fear our own reality. We fear what we are. We fear what God actually created when God willed us into life. We fear the power that God has given us, and we put up barriers in our mind to "protect" us from being a co-creator with God. If you were to ask the flowing woman what could possibly hurt her, she would not answer, because nothing can harm the will of God. Nothing can interfere with what God has created, and what God didn't create, what was made by us, is simply false. It is not real.

As I watched her, the Love she shared expanded, connecting those awakened souls, those minds willing to join, out and beyond the horizon. This place became Heaven, as God had intended. It was always there. It was there, simply covered up by the joke we had made but didn't laugh at. We told this joke about crazy people starving, killing, fucking, eating, getting drunk, and going to war, and a made-up god of hate and anger so weak that we could change its mind simply by thinking, saying, loving, or doing the wrong things. A god that finds joy in sacrifice. A god who tells its creations to put off happiness until you die, be judged worthy because of your sacrifice, and then, just maybe, the god of hate will let you into his perfect world of perfect followers with levels and layers of happiness. A ghost of a god who sits on a throne in some mystical place, surrounded by worshipers who don't even know what they are worshiping.

The god of hate, the smartest guy in the room, with one and only one son, and very easily angered, offering attack, and sending those whom he sees as unworthy not into oblivion, but to be tortured for all eternity. I saw in her the release from the anger at such a god, and the desire to kill that fucker in the clouds. She released me from fear, anger, sadness, loss, sacrifice, guilt, and shame. At least, that's what I thought. But she told me that only I could find revelation from those feelings. All she could do was show me the mistakes I had made.

What I realized as she walked into my awareness is that we cannot ask God to release us from the insanity of this dream of scarcity and fear. She asked, "How can God release you from that which does not exist?" It was a question I had heard many times, but never thought to find an answer for. God cannot take away our fear. Only we can do that, by asking the Holy Spirit to show us what our fears are in reality, which is nothing.

Little children scream and rant when their mothers take away a knife, a gun, or a hammer that might harm them. They have a tantrum and flail around on the floor because they want what they want when they want it. The man in black did that as the flowing woman drew near. Flowers started to grow up around his heeled boots, and vines swirled around the legs of his line of armed men. He barked at his military men to take aim, and they drew their weapons, pointing their guns at the woman walking across the now lush riverbank. He screamed in a high-pitched voice (imagine a four-year-old boy shy of puberty), "Kill that bitch!", and his men opened fire. Not one of the men hesitated, or even blinked.

The bullets flew off towards her but evaporated as they tried to enter her presence. Imagine the bullets leaving the guns, but there wasn't any sound, and none of the bullets made it more than a few inches from the tips of the guns. It's hard to explain, but the man in black became infuriated, screaming at his men to keep firing, to "Kill that fucking bitch before she ruins everything!" When none of his attacks worked, he fell to the ground and kicked his feet, tore at his shirt, and went on and on about how hard he had worked to be in charge, to own the world, and to make the world do his bidding, and here she "waltzes in and destroys all my hopes and dreams."

The beautiful woman cast her gaze towards where the man in black lay on the ground, kicking and screaming in a high-pitched voice, but she didn't look at him directly, or acknowledge him, or even notice him. It was just her survey of Heaven, and her look toward the man in black and his small army turned them to dust that the earth swallowed, and then belched. The man in black and his military were gone in that moment, as though they had never existed, and what I understood was that they had never really existed in God's reality. They were simply an illusion, a projection of insanity, an unreality.

I noticed that the woman was giggling while she floated towards me. Was it you, Epinoia? She looked a little like you, but I couldn't be sure. The last elements of awareness I had of being a separate being, an "other," slipped from me, and what I felt was that Ancient Feeling of Peace that God planted in our minds from the moment of our creation. Tell me, was that you?

"My, me, mine? You, yours, some other, someone we know, someone we don't know…? What are you asking, my beloved? Was I in your dream? Perhaps, if you put my image there. Was I the woman flowing over the great plains? Not in reality. That was all you: the man in black, the people fighting, the army, and the woman. There isn't any other. No separation. Wasn't that the story you were witness to?"

No separation, of course. The knowledge that all power is of God, and what is not of God has no power at all. The separation fallacy surrounded by the belief in a power other than God. The idea of separation, of an "other," is the origin of fear. When I came face-to-face with her, I discovered that we were one, together in God. Not bodies, not split, but — I don't know how to explain it — like water in a river. Like waves of Love. Like threads in a vast cloth. But not like that at all, because to put words to the wordless is an insult and will only offer confusion and distress.

The man in black and his followers believed they had the power to stave off the will of God, but they didn't. The only real power is that of God, of Love, of Forgiveness. Autonomy is a confusing idea, and it is what was driving the men in black. They wanted to be separate and to maintain the illusion of independence. But with that came the fear, anger, and mistrust, which led to attack. They never stopped and simply asked, "Is there another way to look at all of this?" They had nothing to lose by asking. Yet they were convinced they had everything to lose. Their identity was locked in a tight grip of being in control, owning the world, making slaves of everyone they saw, squeezing in their fists a dusty, dying planet not even worth fighting over.

As the woman cast her glance over the dusty, deserted space, she didn't see with the eyes of the ego. She saw what God intended, at least metaphorically. Heaven is formless, so the lush environment I witnessed springing forth from her walking wasn't really there, even though it was what I thought I saw. The men in black, in contrast, were making all their decisions on their own, out of fear of a future that didn't exist, and worried about a past that had never happened. The choice for me was simple: do I pick the Antichrist, or Christ? With the men in black, the world was completely random, chaotic, terrifying, and insane. With the Goddess, the way is clear, peaceful, trusting, and complete.

That was something else I noticed: I made the idea of God complete. Without me, God was left as an open idea, not fulfilled. My reflection of God's Love was essential to the closure of the insanity of the world of the ego. All the Light of the World was generated from me. While the woman was creating the Love of the World, she was humble, yet confident. The men in black, while they orchestrated the insanity of a disordered world, were arrogant in their desire to be little. They asked to be little, and while the flowing woman was offering an extension of what God is offering, and God is offering all there is in all eternity, these angry, hateful men turned their backs and scoffed. They were trading everything for nothing.

How do I call God my friend when you are never there for me? That was the question the man in black was thinking when he evaporated into the earth. He screamed at God, "This is all your doing! You created man in your image, and here you are taking that away. I've done your work to control the sinners of the world. I've forced my Christian ideas out onto the world, but they would not accept my leadership! Why did you lead me astray? Why did you deceive me with your Bibles, and cast judgment over me as a sinner from my inception, only to put me into the ground in favor of some stupid girl?" Then it occurred to me that he was — I was, we all are — angry with God.

His anger was directed towards the sacrifices he had made. Rather than pursuing Love and Joy, he had put that off to control the evil in the world. He had sacrificed God's Love in this so-called life for something much better in the future. Always something better to come, but nothing good about the moment he was in. His thoughts were, *God, I'm terrified of you because I murdered you to take control of the world I projected onto you. I'm angry at you because you have not rewarded my sacrifices that I have offered you now or in the past. Everything I have done is for nothing. It is all lost, and you are the reason for all my losses, so how can I possibly think of you as merciful and loving?*

The answer to his final demand is that God was never his enemy. All God ever asked was for us all to call God our Friend. In that moment, I looked again at the man in black, who for me represented the one I chose to hate rather than love. For him and him alone, I brought hatred into the world and hung onto it long past its value. Ha! Value... It never had any value, never created anything other than more hatred and attack. In that moment — the moment the man in black and his followers were swallowed by what remained of their illusion — I heard God speak. God reminded me that it was never my will to hate or attack anyone or anything, that I was never a prisoner to fear or a slave to death. I was never a little creature crawling around on a dusty planet. I had made it all up to hide from the Truth I feared.

What was true? The Light in Heaven shines only for me, the child of God. God had one child, and we are all that child. In that instant, I had forgiven God. I saw the man in black not as an enemy, but as a mistake, and a brother in love, and by doing that, my will and God's Will were finally aligned, and I was no longer afraid of God's Will. The man in black was an idol. He was a limit in my mind, as are all idols. They are the walls that block us from uncovering our true identity. The man in black was a belief in a form that

I mistakenly thought could bring me happiness. It was me saying, "I have no need for everything, when I can have this little thing for just a moment and it will be everything to me." God said to me that all I ever needed to do was to decide in favor of the Truth, and everything would be given to me. Not in the form, but in the formless. Not as little strips of paper and discs of metal. Not in machines, or stuff, but in reality, which is beyond any form.

I was being content with small ideas, my tiny insane ideas that were of no value to anyone or anything other than to keep us locked in a nightmare of madness. God's wholeness has no form because it is unlimited. Any form, whether a body, a place, or an object, is a limit. It is a prison. It makes our minds small and incomplete. And completion is our function as a Child of God. We complete God by accepting God's Will. Something that I need to tell you is that God's Will is a memory. It is recognizable. It is simple in its grace and perfection.

There was a gap I had made that I filled with toys that caused worry. None of the toys I had made would last, and my fear was of dying and leaving everything behind, and being judged, and not knowing for sure if I had lived correctly, or had shared my toys well enough, or had loved the right people. None of these toys ever brought me joy. The entire mountain that was taken from me. The sense of wholeness from being raped. The sense of security when a priest told me that I was a child worthy only of hell and damnation. The gap was not there, even though I thought it was. What was true was that I was dreaming of idols, rather than accepting the Truth of God.

For so many lifetimes, I had held onto the idea that sins had occurred, that God was looking down on us as sinners. And my salvation, our salvation, is a paradox in that I was forgiving that which had never happened. I know it sounds absurd, but forgiveness was dependent on my overlooking stuff nobody ever actually did. I might watch a person kill someone in the streets and think it was real or watch a news broadcast and think how awful the event was, and proclaim it to have happened, and judge it a sin. But it was simply my own mistake in judgment. All I could do when I realized what God was telling me was True, when I could hear God's Voice clearly, was to offer forgiveness. It's funny — I had always thought that I needed to understand the truth before I could offer forgiveness. But I had that backwards. I had to forgive first, and only then understand, because in my forgiveness, reality was revealed to me, and only then could understanding happen. In other words, it was impossible for me to understand anything, because I was covering reality with the veil of sinfulness. Does that make sense?

Epinoia said, "It makes perfect sense, my beloved. When you were seeing an enemy in your Brothers and Sisters, you would not see them for who they are in reality. And you could not accept God's Love until you forgave that which had never actually happened. Understanding only comes to an open mind. When your mind was cluttered with anger, hatred, fear, guilt, and shame, it was impossible to understand anything."

Yes, I was placing meaning on what I chose to look out and see. I remember wondering how I could turn a blind eye to what was right in front of me. As a little kid, a friend of mine stole some candy from a store. I watched him do it and felt deep guilt, because he did it for me, to earn my friendship. I witnessed him taking the candy, putting it in his pocket, and walking out of the store. He gave it to me on the street, and I ate it. Those things I saw with my own two eyes, and I held onto that guilt for many years. Except it wasn't true. That is the enigma of forgiveness: overlooking what I think I saw and replacing that thought with the thought guided by the Holy Spirit. When I am in alignment with the Holy Spirit, making decisions and allowing any judgment to come from the Holy Spirit, only then is it possible to see beyond what seems to be obvious.

That was the moment I finally, at long last, decided that I no longer want idols. I can still see them, but I do not believe in them, nor do I want them any longer. An ancient hatred thus passed on from my mind, and the loving woman looked directly into my face. Her eyes were warm and inviting, and her expression was absolutely peaceful. She reached out her hand, and at that moment, I knew I was taking the hand of Christ, and the Love of Christ was being accepted, and once that was done came the knowledge of God-Love, which I simply cannot explain in words or expressions. The idols I had sought had never offered anything to me other than guilt. None of it had ever given me, or anyone I had ever met, anything of any value.

For a moment, I was paired with the final thoughts of the man in black, and the question that came to mind was, *To what end?* The struggles, deceit, conflict, and acquisition of what the ego looks on as abundance — what was it all for? It was temporary, and once one thing was acquired, then the next was desired, and on and on. The price was too high, and we all pay it together. None of it was paid for by anyone alone.

As I sat quietly with the knowledge I had accepted, Epinoia said, "One more thing before we move on, my beloved. Tell me what you experienced with specific grievances. You had touched on rape, murder, stealing candy, telling lies, and many other moments of attack. These are all very specific encounters. How did you get through all those experiences? The mirrors were all gone except one, and that one was the culmination of all the others, and yet that one is also gone now. How did you sift through all the 'sins' of man?"

Then Epinoia said, "The true Will of God rests in hands that are joined. When our minds are one, we see God as our Savior. Before that happens, God is the enemy, wanting to punish us for our so-called sin of separation. Your will, my will, God's Will — they are all one will, connected, co-creating Love. There is so much happiness in being wrong about everything. It is the greatest relief to be wrong about the Love of God, and the mercy is in the forgiveness we provide in the gap outside of Heaven, knowing that once forgiveness is complete, it is no longer necessary."

Now, for me, it is in the universality of the vision of Christianity. It came as a look of general despair being healed all at once with one blessing. The ego looks at Christ as the anointed one, or the person next in line to take the throne of God. But the true vision of Christ is a universal acceptance of forgiveness. That's how I got through it, and how I'll remain healed.

Chapter 20.

One More Time (the Quickest Path is Not Always the Easiest)

Epinoia said, "Still, for you, my loving child, there is a class ahead that you will want to attend. There is still a mirror in your magic space that would benefit from your attention. It is not a mirror that has been experienced before. But it is necessary, nonetheless. At this moment, you still see me as a separate being. You see the Holy Spirit as an entity that is a higher power than you. Compared to God, to the Christ, to Jesus, and even to me, you see yourself as smaller, less powerful, and not as worthy or gifted. That will change given time, and you will find out very quickly within that next mirror who you really are, and you will bring together an entire sisterhood and brotherhood. Jesus once wondered what it would be like if ten million people all came to the Light at once. This mirror is a way for that to happen, and your role is to bring them together. For a moment, you will be gifted with more, and they less, but as the teaching and learning come together, you will all be the same. Teaching and learning are the same. It goes on in our waking hours, and it continues when we sleep. This mirror is about demonstrating the Love of God.

"It is time to redefine what Christianity means. To the ego, the Christ is connected to the anointed one and is offered as the Christ Jesus. But Jesus isn't the only Christ, and Christ is not Jesus' last name, and he isn't the only person to hold the vision of Christ. The vision of Christ is universal. It is for everyone, not just for Jesus. This life journey waiting for you will offer proof of that, and there are many millions of seemingly separate souls ready to come together with the Love of God, and extend God's Love, and shine a light into the darkness of the ego. This will end the myths of the ego mind; science is a myth, religion is a myth, and the crucifixion is a myth as well. For so long, the focus has allowed the ego to use guilt to uphold its desires and remain in a position of leadership. Well, you can call it leadership, but it isn't in Truth.

"As a teacher of Christ, your curriculum will be given to you and determined by what you think you are in line with the Holy Spirit. At this moment, you have come to realize you are an extension of God, and that Love will carry you through this life. You may wonder if you are God's gift, and the answer is yes, you are. You are God's Gift, as are we all. Your adventure, hand in hand with the Holy Spirit, will reinforce what you have come to believe about yourself. These experiences in the Borderland that we have forgiven are the basis for eliminating any self-doubt."

"But Epinoia," I said, "I don't need or want to go back. I can feel the fear building up at the idea of being a body again. I'm not a body, and the freedom that comes with that knowledge is too attractive to let go of, even for an instant. Tell me you're kidding. Tell me I can finish my education here, in the gap, in the Borderland."

"My sweet child, of course, you will never be forced to do anything. And yes, you can complete your mission here in the Borderland. But I know your soul intimately, and I know you want to return home as soon as possible. This is the fastest way home. It is the path being offered by the Holy Spirit. This mirror is in perfect alignment with God, and each decision you make will be made together with God, so there is nothing to fear. Take your time, my beloved, and sit with the path presented. Know that it is coming directly from the Holy Spirit. Stand in front of the mirror and see how you feel about what it represents. If you have any misgivings, then decide to take a pass until you're ready. But if you see in that mirror the connection to a life of goodwill and love, as I know you will, perhaps you will take this final step home. There is nothing to decide at this moment, but keep in mind, we are still talking in terms of time and space. You are still hearing me, and you are still asking for my guidance. We are not One Mind quite yet, my dearest love." And she giggled.

Chapter 21.

Should I Stay or Should I Go?

My mind went blank for what seemed like a long while, and I contemplated everything that I had been through. The fear I had felt when she told me that I had another mirror yet to discover slipped from my mind, and I allowed the Holy Spirit to talk to me. The meditative state I found myself in was filled with God-Love and peace. Off in the distance, I could see the shining mirror. It was completely white with the light of God. Unlike the other mirrors — which were all gone now — this shimmering mirror of light was much different. There were no veils covering it, no shadows or grievances. The reflection was complete calmness, and there wasn't a robed body in front of it, either. Simple elegance. Graceful. This mirror wasn't magic like the others.

As I got closer, I could see that there were no surprises, no battles, no conflicts. It was perfect God-Love held in a space built around a simple form. If I were to take this final step, I would be the Light of the World I would enter. My decisions would all be in alignment with God-Love, so there would be no fear, no pain of any kind, no grievances, no shame, no guilt, no attacks, no defense, but only perfect Love. Things would still happen in an ego sense, but I would not believe them or be bound to them emotionally.

It became instantly clear that this wasn't a decision I could stay away from, because it was my destiny. I could see immediately that Epinoia was correct about this being the fastest path to Heaven. It would be a life in a body, but my desires in this life would be in alignment with the Holy Spirit, and I would be a teacher of God. Not like a schoolteacher, offering something to others who had less than me and I was bestowing knowledge on to them, but instead, the emphasis would be on teaching as a constant process, from birth to the point at which I would set the body aside. Teaching would be to learn, as I would be teaching not just others, but also myself; it would all be one and the same.

It would be a life of demonstration, and from that demonstration of peace and love, others would learn, but so would I. We are all always teaching; there is simply no way not to teach. What I would be teaching on this journey would be the Love of God, and in perfect alignment with the Holy Spirit. Not as a preacher or a priest — God knows we do not need any more of those — but as an example, so that my calm and peaceful mind would touch other minds, and like gentle ripples in a pond, it would echo out across the entire population, and then out into the Universe, singing the song of Love scripted by God and echoed by the Holy Spirit.

All bodies are teaching and learning devices, and their purpose is to allow us to communicate forgiveness, which is not necessary in Heaven. My choices in this body experience would be to choose with God, and to teach with the Holy Spirit. The curriculum we teach is always based on what we think we are, and in this case, I would be an extension of God, and would complete God's original idea of a perfect Child. Does that make sense at all? The teaching I would be set on would be to remove any doubt in who and what I am, what we all are, in perfect reality. God is perfect Love, and so are all of us, because we were created by God. Perfection can only create perfection.

We have for so long tried in every way to convince ourselves that we are not perfect, that only God is perfect, and we are all sinners, destined to be judged as failures. This is the lie of guilt that the ego lives on. Without that simple mistake — which is not a sin, but only a mistake — the ego could not exist. What we think is real is what we teach, and by teaching what we think of as real, we make it more real for ourselves. What we plant in our minds grows because we give it attention and nurture it. This can be a mistake based on the fear of the ego, or the reality of the Love of God; that is our choice. This life path would be one of complete confidence and offer only the Love of God.

This so-called life, or adventure in a body, or trip to the school of flesh, would be to choose again and to show that the Love of God is always available. Without teachers of God, there is little hope of salvation. The world of sin would go on seemingly forever, and the god of hate and hell would also seem real and beyond any doubt. By the way, a teacher of God is anyone who chooses to be one. They are not ordained by some religious authority. My only qualification in this new life is that I would be making the deliberate choice to see my interests as exactly the same as everyone else's. Because I have made that decision, now my entire life path would be clear and established by God and carried out daily through the Holy Spirit. The call is universal and always there. God is always talking to us, giving us direction. The problem is, we listen for the words of the ego, which God doesn't understand. Instead, in this journey, I would be perfectly connected to the Love of God, and God's voice of Love would extend through me in every moment.

When we follow the curriculum of God through the Holy Spirit, the time saved is immeasurable. In every lifetime, even those that seem to be only of sin and completely disastrous, there is a glimmer of the Love of God. When we are caught up in those moments, we may not be able to see the Love of God, but it is there. In this lifetime, that glimmer would become unmistakable, and it would bring time to an end. That power would be placed in my hands through the grace of God. Time has an ending, and it is that ending that as a teacher of God I would be here to bring about.

The pupils I would be assigned would be selected by God based on our universal understanding. They would seek me out the moment I was born, and together we would bring about the end of the ego time. It is not up to us to decide the course of study on our own. The only decision we make is when we want to learn what God has to offer. And this life gathering would be with those who are all ready to accept the Truth, and it would be ours because we have already learned that Truth together. We would all share one interest and one goal. We would all see in each other that our interests are all one and the same. Because of this, the need for argument and conflict would be absent. There may be millions of us, each with our own seemingly special problems, but we would come to realize there is only one answer, one solution, and that is the alignment of our will with God.

I could see in this mirror my true self, the self that God had created. Not as a body, but free, as God had created me. Each encounter would appear to be superficial — casual encounters and chance meetings with apparent strangers that would become moments of salvation. The ego would tell you that these encounters cannot exist in reality, that you must always be on guard, because those you encounter are there to do you harm. But I could see in this mirror that the Love of God was arranging all my moments in perfect Love, so I would be able to place complete trust in those encounters and know that salvation and the end of time are at hand.

The end of time is not iconic. It is not a time to fear, nor is it a time of exclusivity. What I could see in this mirror is that the end of time will be universal, and a time of perfect forgiveness. It is a moment to be cherished and looked forward to. It is a time of Trust. Trust is the foundation on which my ability to fulfill this life purpose would depend. Its basis is complete Trust in God. This new world can be trusted because it is not governed by the laws of the ego, or what we call "man." Instead, it is governed by the power within us, which is offered as an extension of God's Love for us. It became clear as I looked into this mirror that the experience would make it impossible to place my trust in the petty ideas of the ego ever again. There would never be any doubt about my goal. Events would take place, and I would witness them with the eyes of the Holy Spirit, overlooking the absurdity and seeing the Love of God in its place.

The culmination of these so-called lifetimes was a period of undoing the ego. I experienced them as painful, but they didn't need to be painful. The experiences in the Borderland with Epinoia had been a period of sorting out what I thought of as important from what is actually important. Along with that, there was a period of relinquishing that which is no longer of any value. For me, this had the effect in many lifetimes of me giving up what I thought of as desirable. But I came to understand that none of it was of any value at all. Slips of paper, shiny objects, even relationships that were battered with a multitude of emotions were only there to cause pain. For me, this was followed by a time of seeming peacefulness, like a plateau; I felt in some lifetimes like I was on a quiet vacation. What I had not come to terms with was that I didn't fully know what was valuable and what was valueless. I had thought that a quiet life was set up by having enough money and few obstacles, so that I could go along in what seemed like a lavish lifestyle. Much of what I went through in the Borderland was unsettling because I learned just how wrong I was. There was great joy in uncovering my mistakes and forgiving them, but the experience was very unsettling, to be sure.

Chapter 22.

Bringing it All Together

This next life would be a life of achievement. Not in the ego sense; not with great wealth, fame, and conquering. The achievement would be the consolidation of the learning that brings forth complete peace of mind. And where would we go from there, when complete peace is already ours? That is one of the questions this lifetime would uncover for me and the Universe I would enter.

All that remained was for me to step fully in front of the mirror and take the form being offered. Trust in the process, Trust in God, and from that Trust would spring complete honesty and the ability to become the Light of the World — the Second Coming, as it were. To the ego mind, this sounds arrogant. That's because the second coming has been depicted as Jesus coming back to judge the world and cast out those bad people that God made, but whom he didn't think worked out so well. Jesus would come back angry, carrying a sword to hack up anyone he found to be unforgivable. I imagine it might sound to some like I think I might be going back to start slashing the bad guys and lifting up the good guys. But that's not at all what I mean.

The true arrogance lies in thinking that we're small little people who don't deserve God's Love, and therefore we are convinced that we need to be judged for our sins. But making sins real is the mistake. When I say the Second Coming, think of me being a cleanup crew manager. I'm stepping into this mirror merely to correct mistakes and help us return to sanity. Read that as my helping myself return to sanity, because I've been completely nuts for way too long. The purpose of the entire process is to end the teaching of the Holy Spirit. You see, now that seems arrogant, too — like I have the power to end the teaching of the great and powerful Oz or something. But the Second Coming will shine light (my light, in this case) on everything as One thing. God is simple, and the ego has done everything it can to make it complicated. God only counts to One. That's it — end of story. There is only One.

This event or experience is one in which time cannot affect us at all. Time and the ego have no power here, for every life and death that I imagined in the past will be completely released from those dreams. When in one life I called myself a saint and told others what to do, as if I were the god of hate and cast a living hell on everyone I encountered, that wasn't a sin. It wasn't real. Forgiveness is releasing us from that which did not happen. Also, when I was raped and tied to a bed and died in the rapist's semen and the excrement of my little body, those grievances will be let go as well. The heavy fog the ego has placed over our eyes will be lifted. By me. And by you, my beloved.

The Second Coming needs our eyes to see, our feet to walk with our sisters and brothers, our hands and voices to offer Love, and most of all, our willingness to carry out God's Will. I will offer proof that God's Will can be done, and we will rejoice together in the Second Coming. Of course, the ego will say, "Hopefully we will rejoice, but don't get your hopes up..." But my final visit would be used to prove that we no longer need hope. Hope is the expectation and desire for certain things to happen. My Second Coming would be the relinquishment of hope, because there isn't any hope in Heaven. It simply isn't necessary. And yes, together, we will move mountains.

I stepped in front of the mirror and took the form it offered — the form I chose. This was my decision. I won't describe the form to you because my description would be an insult to the absolute beauty and grace this happy dream was offering. What I will say is, you will recognize the form the moment you see It. This is a form that is not dependent on age, although I would start as what we think of as a baby and grow into an adult. The experiences of the ego life would not be lost on me, or even changed. What would be different in this life is how I see those events as unreal, and the Love of God would flow through me to everyone I encounter, no matter their intentions.

Try not to imagine a mental picture but allow the Holy Spirit to offer an image to you in the silence of a deep meditation. As you do, remind yourself: we are not bodies; we are free; we are as God created us. So, any image I would project would be counterintuitive. What's important is what happened next, in a Holy Instant.

Chapter 23.

A Born-Again Christian? (Ugh, Just Don't Tell Anyone)

My soon-to-be mother lay in her bed. Her water had broken hours before, and while she was contracting rapidly now, she was not in pain. My father was at her side, encouraging her gently. It's funny — as my spirit hovered over them, I could see everything as if there were light coming from within. Nothing was held in shadow, and each person in the room with my mother was Holy and expressing the Love of God. The midwives were quiet and supportive, and it was as if they knew how important this journey would be for me and for them. The room looked like a bedroom, but I knew it was a hospital. Imagine an upscale hotel room, and you'll be in the right place.

One of the midwives said, "It won't be long now, sweetheart, just breathe and push. Your lovely child is about to enter this world. There is nothing to worry about. You're healthy, your baby is healthy, and there is love here."

The two midwives worked in unison, as if in a well-rehearsed dance. Think of the Scrambler ride at a carnival, but in slow motion. Each midwife acted like she was connected to spindles as the center rotated around the room, coming close to each other, yet going about their roles without ever bumping into each other. Many years past, their teacher would often say, "It's never okay to drop the baby. You must act with complete grace." And that is exactly what they did.

Unlike in the last lifetime, this time I felt complete confidence in my decision. I was here with the will of God and the Holy Spirit, and together, we would bring about the Second Coming. I wasn't running from anything; I was stepping toward the Love of God. In this moment, I wasn't trying to hide or forget. I was here to remember the Love of God and share that Love with everyone I would encounter. In all my previous so-called lives, I had been bouncing, like a ball on a Bolo bat, or a paddleball. It was as though I would jump from one life experience to another without thinking, and then pretend that it was all happening *to* me, rather than something I had chosen. The difference now is that I was in a room with parents I had projected, with midwives I had made up, and for an experience I was looking forward to.

Many lifetimes ago, Whispering Winds told me a story. He said that the dimple under our noses, the philtrum, is there because God was silencing our memories. Just before we are born into this world, he said, God casts his thumb over our mouths to quiet our remembrance of our previous lives, so we can start afresh. Many mystics and shamans have stories they tell about how a broad or narrow philtrum can impact the life of the person. On the contrary, scientists will tell you the lip dimple is caused by genetics and that it doesn't have any function in humans today but was once perhaps a way to enhance our sense of smell. But we're all just making that up. My baby form was born with a philtrum, but I didn't forget anything I had learned from my experiences in the Borderland. When I entered this world, the body I projected was perfectly formed.

I didn't cry. When one of the midwives pinched my nipple, I giggled. She made a surprised expression, but let it pass. One of them asked my father if he would like to cut the umbilical cord, and he did so without any hesitation. After a short examination, my mother breathed deeply as I was placed on her chest, our skin making contact as her arms wrapped around me. I nursed right away and was in a wide-awake state.

My father rested on the side of the bed, and the three of us lay together. My mother said, "Do you hear music? I hear music, like a distant memory. It's lovely."

My father said, "I hear it, too. Is it coming from her? It sounds like it's coming from her."

My mother said, "She's so beautiful. Her complexion — is she glowing a little? She looks like she's glowing!"

My father: "I noticed that, too. It's pretty. I've never seen anything like it." Turning towards the midwives, he asked, "Is that normal?"

One of the midwives came over and looked closely. "She's perfectly healthy. Nothing to worry about. She is perfectly safe."

My father kissed me, and then kissed my mother. "What shall we call her?"

Without any hesitation, my mother said, "She is Epinoia. Soulfulness and deep wisdom."

My father said, "Yes, Epinoia. That seems right to me, too."

About the Author

I have often said there was nothing wrong with my childhood that 30+ years of counseling wouldn't cure. What I hadn't realized is it would require three visits to intensive mental health facilities, one of which lasted more than six weeks. Boy, I could tell you stories, and in fact, it's why I decided to write about forgiveness, recovery, and spirituality. My desire is to tell stories, not just about my own experiences, but about the human condition in general.

I have spent the better part of my life coming to terms with the abuses I've experienced. Everything from sexual, physical, educational, spiritual, and emotional, all built up like a leaking container that caused me to look inside to find healing and forgiveness. I say forgiveness because after spending time with a lot of very smart and caring psychologists, I came to the notion that I needed to find forgiveness for what is basically unforgivable.

My time spent in recovery and across the desk from psychologists ended when my last therapist told me I should get an honorary doctorate because I knew about as much as he did at that point in time. He said: "Mark, you will have to find your way on your own. The only difference between the two of us currently is which side of the desk we're on."

I spent the next couple of decades meditating, studying, and developing a deep understanding of my inner self. Not inside my body, but inside my mind.